"Hey, are you going to be all right on this one?

"I know it hits close to home," Miguel sympathized.

"When have you ever known me not to be all right?" Madeline said. No matter how challenging things got, she never let anything personal keep her from doing her job.

"What we do is tough. It's natural if a case gets to us sometimes."

"I should be asking how you're doing after everything that's happened recently."

"I'm guessing your deflection means I struck a nerve."

More like an old wound that healed a little each time she rescued a child.

"You know, you never answered my question."

"I'm fine." She'd joined the FBI to become a kidnapping expert. Sure, whenever they got a case like this, it burned Madeline's gut that another innocent child had been snatched, but this was what she lived for.

A chance to save a young life and spare a family an agonizing loss.

She was going to do everything in her power to bring Emma Rhodes home.

TRACING A KIDNAPPER

Juno Rushdan

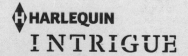

HARLEQUIN
INTRIGUE

To my patient husband and understanding children, thank you
for your love and support that made writing this book possible.

Special thanks and acknowledgment are given to Juno Rushdan
for her contribution to the Behavioral Analysis Unit miniseries.

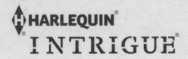

INTRIGUE

Recycling programs
for this product may
not exist in your area.

ISBN-13: 978-1-335-55527-4

Tracing a Kidnapper

Copyright © 2021 by Harlequin Books S.A.

For questions and comments about the quality of this book,
please contact us at CustomerService@Harlequin.com.

Harlequin Enterprises ULC
22 Adelaide St. West, 40th Floor
Toronto, Ontario M5H 4E3, Canada
www.Harlequin.com

Printed in U.S.A.

Juno Rushdan is the award-winning author of steamy, action-packed romantic thrillers that keep you on the edge of your seat. She writes about kick-ass heroes and strong heroines fighting for their lives as well as their happily-ever-afters. As a veteran air force intelligence officer, she uses her background supporting Special Forces to craft realistic stories that make you sweat and swoon. Juno currently lives in the DC area with her patient husband, two rambunctious kids and a spoiled rescue dog. To receive a FREE book from Juno, sign up for her newsletter at junorushdan.com/mailing-list. Also be sure to follow Juno on BookBub for the latest on sales at bit.ly/BookBubJuno.

Books by Juno Rushdan

Harlequin Intrigue

Tracing a Kidnapper

A Hard Core Justice Thriller

Hostile Pursuit
Witness Security Breach
High-Priority Asset
Innocent Hostage
Unsuspecting Target

Visit the Author Profile page at Harlequin.com.

CAST OF CHARACTERS

Madeline Striker—As the Behavioral Analysis Unit's kidnapping expert, this special agent is put in charge when the six-year-old daughter of a high-profile businessman goes missing. This is her toughest assignment due to her tragic past of losing her own sister, who was kidnapped at the same age and never found.

Jackson Rhodes—Devoted single father and newly named CEO of Emerald Technology Corp. He's made a lot of enemies over the years because of his success in business, but he can't fathom why anyone would kidnap his little girl.

Emma Rhodes—Jackson's six-year-old daughter.

Andrew Phillips—Vice President of ETC, he has an ax to grind with Jackson and the most to gain from Emma's kidnapping, but would he really go that far?

Miguel Peters—Supervisory agent of the BAU, he's the team's counterterrorism expert.

Nicholas James—BAU profiler focused on serial killers. He's the only person on the team who knows how difficult this case is for Madeline.

Dashiell West—BAU cybercrimes specialist. He always finds something that others miss.

Prologue

Organized chaos. The only way to describe Corporate Family Day, Jackson thought.

"Daddy," Emma said, coming up to him and interrupting the chairman midsentence. "There's a puppy. I want to go see it."

"Just a second, sweetheart." Jackson patted his six-year-old on the shoulder.

"She is so adorable, dressed in that little pantsuit," the chairman said.

Emma beamed. "I wanted to be twinsies with Daddy." She looked at Jackson. "I have to hurry if I want to pet the puppy."

His assistant, Brittany Hall, had hired a magician and had mentioned an animal in the act, but he thought it was a bunny.

"Please, Daddy." Her blond curls framed her angelic face and her brown eyes sparkled with determination that'd one day serve her well. "It's right over there." She pointed to the atrium, but Jackson couldn't see anything through the crowd.

The space was jam-packed with two hundred Emerald Technology Corp employees along with their kids and spouses.

"Patience. We'll see it together. Go grab a bite to eat." This day was already testing his multi-tasking skills in new ways; he didn't need Emma having a hangry meltdown, too.

With a deflated look that pinched something in his chest, she trudged over to the catered food on the table.

The chairman cleared his throat, drawing Jackson's attention. "As I was saying, our current stock prices reflect the fact that the board made an excellent decision with you."

"It was an honor to be chosen as CEO." Jackson pulled on a smile. At the job, he gave one hundred percent, but when he was with Emma, she was his number-one priority. He hated making her wait.

"There's someone I'd like you to speak with." The chairman gestured for a woman to come over. "Her son wants to meet you. A teenager who is a big admirer."

"Certainly." Jackson turned to get Emma for introductions, but she was no longer at the table. He glanced around the room. "Emma?" Through a break in the crowd he caught a glimpse of the atrium. The magician was speaking with Brittany, but he didn't see Emma. "Excuse me a moment. My little girl has wandered off." He stepped away, searching the conference room, checked every chair, corner, even under the table.

Jackson cut through the crowd into the atrium and looked for a gaggle of kids who'd be drawn to a cute puppy, but everyone was milling about, chatting. Unease churned in his gut.

Brittany came up to him. "The band just arrived. Bouncy castle and face painters are outside in the courtyard. Plenty of arts and crafts Emma will love."

Jackson looked around past her. "Have you seen her? Is she in the courtyard?"

"I just came from there. We haven't opened it up to everyone yet. Maybe she's eating."

"She's not in the conference room. I think she took off to see a puppy. Does the magician have one?"

Brittany shook her head. "Only a bunny for the show. I haven't seen any other pets."

Cold dread swept through him, but he pushed it aside. He was surrounded by hardworking employees, good people who had their kids there. This was a safe place.

"Take a look in the restroom," he said, "and I'll check with security at the front."

"Okay." Brittany hurried down the hall.

Jackson ran to the security desk. "Has Emma passed by here?" All the guards knew his daughter. Each one had complimented her on her outfit, which had made her grin with delight.

"No, sir. She hasn't come this way and she certainly hasn't gone through the front door."

His mind raced as he hurried back into the atrium where the conference room was.

"She wasn't there," Brittany said, rushing to him. "No one inside has seen her."

A sinking, hollow sensation spread in the pit of his stomach.

Where are you, honey? Jackson clasped the back of his neck and rubbed the tension gathering there. "Everyone! I need your attention." The crowd quieted. All eyes turned to him. "I can't find my daughter, Emma. She's six, blonde, wearing a blue pantsuit. Look around you. If you see her, call out." She had to be here. He'd looked away from her for a minute. Thirty seconds. Less.

Heads turned on a swivel. A murmur rippled through the crowd. Jackson waited and waited, clenching his jaw against the suffocating pressure building in his chest. The mutter of voices withered and died. Parents clutched their own young kids closer. Compassionate gazes found his as every nerve ending burned with terrible certainty.

No one had found Emma because she was gone.

Jackson took out his cell phone and dialed 911.

Chapter One

"Stop whatever you're doing." Supervisory Special Agent Miguel Peters poked his head in Special Agent Madeline Striker's small office. His designer suit and dark stubble gave him a deceptively suave air, but he was tough and no-nonsense. "I need to brief everyone now."

Without further elaboration, he strode down the hall, rounding everyone else up. The team's communications liaison with the local police, Caitlyn Yang, was hot on his heels.

Madeline logged off her computer, anticipating that one or more of them would be headed out the door once the emergency meeting was done. Sometimes the ops tempo was fast and furious, and they had to be ready at a moment's notice. Grabbing a notepad and pen, she stood, facing fellow Special Agent Nicholas James, who'd stopped in her doorway.

"I wonder what type of bomb just dropped," Nick said.

There was no telling. At the Behavioral Analysis Unit—BAU—they handled the gamut from serial killers, explosives, cybercrimes, fraud, counterterrorism to kidnapping—Madeline's specialty.

"No doubt the ugly kind." The kind that kept her awake most nights and pushed her to work twelve-, sometimes sixteen-hour days, but there was no need to mention that.

Being a part of the BAU took a toll on all of them. Though they each had their personal reasons for doing the job.

Tall with an athletic build, Nick walked alongside her to the large conference room in the Bureau's Seattle headquarters.

Madeline entered the sleek boardroom, where Liam McDare, their tech guru, already had slides set up on the large digital screen for the briefing. Hands down, he was the best and quickest at research and compiling data.

Flicking a glance at the oversize FBI logo on the wall, Madeline pulled out a leather chair next to Caitlyn as Dashiell West—Dash, as everyone called him—hustled inside the room, followed by David Dyson, the office intern and Nick's protégé.

"This is time sensitive." Miguel spoke from the head of the table before everyone had a chance to sit. When Director Olivia Branson traveled, which was often, he filled in for her. "We have a child abduction case. An hour ago, the daughter of Jackson Rhodes, the new CEO for Emerald Technology Corp, was reported missing."

Madeline's stomach clenched like a fist. Almost half a million children went missing every year, but landing this type of case got to her each time.

Everyone's attention flickered to her, but she focused on Miguel's intense gaze. He tended to defer to the agent with the most relevant expertise for the investigation to take the lead once in the field.

This one would be hers. It was something she dreaded but was also eager to tackle. She wouldn't let him down. "What do we know so far?" she asked.

Miguel gestured for Liam to start the slideshow. An image of a handsome man holding a little girl came up on the screen. "This is Emma Rhodes with her father. The girl was kidnapped at ETC's annual Corporate Family Day event. She's only six years old."

Madeline ignored the quick chill that sprinted up her spine as she stiffened in her seat.

Six. The same age as her sister when she'd been kidnapped twenty-three years ago. Madeline had been eight. They'd gotten off the school bus and had stopped at the playground on their way home. One minute her sister had been there and the next she was gone.

After an exhaustive search, she was never found. No suspects had been arrested. No closure for their family.

Madeline looked up and met Nick's gaze, his green eyes assessing her. He turned away as if he'd been caught staring.

"Anything on the company's surveillance feed?" Dash, the team's cybercrimes specialist, asked.

"Nada." Miguel shook his head. "Every video camera that could've captured someone speaking with the girl or taking her was disabled."

"The timing of the abduction at the event," Madeline said, thinking aloud, "and disabling the cameras indicates this was premeditated. Someone planned and waited for the right moment when no one would notice."

"How many people were at the event?" Nick asked.

"It was loud, crowded and quite busy." Caitlyn tucked a lock of long black hair behind an ear as she scrolled through her phone for an answer. Her point of contact with the local police texted her with information as soon as they received it, updating her in almost real time. "A hundred and fifteen employees and catering staff, but that number doesn't include all the other kids or spouses." She looked up from her phone. "No one can even say for certain if every employee was present."

Madeline made a note. "Any demands?"

"None so far," Miguel said.

Not unusual in the early stages, but the first seventy-two hours were critical. As time went on there were fewer bread crumbs to follow. "What do we know about the parents?" Madeline asked.

Most kids were taken by a noncustodial parent, a family member or acquaintance. It was very rare for it to be a stranger. That only happened in less than one percent of missing children cases, but in those instances, it was even more crucial for them to work fast because the child could be in imminent danger.

Liam toggled to the next slide, bringing up a picture of Jackson in a polo shirt and shorts. Thick blond hair, blue eyes, tanned, the sculpted body of a Greek god with a face to match. Classically shaped features and a chiseled jaw. A haughty expression like he was prepared to conquer the world.

"Born and raised in Seattle," Miguel said, filling in the background information. "Business degree from Harvard. MBA from Wharton. He climbed the ranks quickly at Emerald Technology Corp and beat out stiff competition to be named CEO last month at thirty-four."

Madeline had gone to school at Yale and knew the type: an elitist golden boy born with a silver spoon in his mouth who never even had a bad hair day. WASP credentials came with lineage and the right connections. "Does he come from money? Have a trust fund?"

Whether a kidnapper's motive was money or notoriety, millionaires and high-profile executives proved to be tempting targets for abduction. Kidnapping insurance was a big deal for a reason.

"Nope." Liam advanced to an article on Jackson in *Cascadia Business* magazine. "According to this, he comes from a middle-income family. Received financial aid, student loans, and worked while in school to pay the rest of his tuition."

The same as Madeline. Ivy League institutions didn't offer academic or athletic scholarships. Getting a degree felt like a full-time job, but the hard work paid lifelong dividends for the top-notch education.

Taking a deep breath, she took another look at Jackson Rhodes. In the picture featured in the article he wore an impeccably tailored suit. His smile was bright and flawless, but this time she spotted the hint of sadness in his eyes. There was far more to him beneath the surface. "What about the mother? Do we know anything about their relationship? Hostile divorce? Nasty custody battle? Trouble of any sort? Or are they happily married?"

"Francesca Hyltin-Rhodes is deceased," Miguel said as Liam advanced to the next slide. "She was a principal ballerina in the Pacific

Northwest Ballet company until she got sick. She died of cancer when Emma was two. Jackson has raised his daughter on his own for the past four years. The magazine article described him as a doting father."

How awful for a child to lose a parent so young. It must've been hard for Jackson to raise her alone. Despite the rough patches, Madeline's parents were still together, and she couldn't imagine her father trying to cope on his own when she had been little.

Madeline stared at a photo of Francesca and Jackson, him standing behind her, with his arms wrapped around her, his hands resting on her pregnant belly. *Beautiful.* A picture-perfect couple. Emma favored her father, but she had her mother's eyes. "Other family members?"

Liam shook his head. "There are no living relatives on either side."

"Abductions by strangers are the rarest type of cases of missing children, and even then," Madeline said, "the kids are usually taken as the child is going to or from school. In this situation with a new executive who's received a lot of recent media attention, I think the girl is alive and that the father will get ransom demands. Soon. The kidnapper targeted Emma Rhodes specifically for a reason."

Caitlyn's cell phone buzzed. She picked it up, swiped through on her screen and looked at a message. "Madeline, you must be psychic. My point of contact with the police on-site said the father just received ransom demands. He must step down as CEO within twenty-four hours if he ever wants to see his daughter again."

Dash let out a low whistle that underscored the surprise etched on everyone's face. "Maybe an ETC employee who isn't too happy about Jackson's promotion took the girl."

Miguel nodded as if thinking the same. "Or a rival at another company."

"Did the police say anything about the caller's voice?" Madeline leaned back in her seat, drumming her fingers on the arm of the chair. "Male, female, the tone used?"

"There wasn't a call." Caitlyn set her phone down. "The father received the demands via text."

Madeline froze. "Text?" Now, *that* was unusual. Jackson Rhodes wouldn't have a cell number that was easy to obtain. Not that it would stop a determined person, but something about the kidnapper sending a text rather than making a call bothered her.

"All right," Miguel said. "Madeline, you're the lead on this. I want everyone to head over to the scene and pitch in any way you can."

Everyone rose and gathered their things.

"It's good we didn't have a Family Day here to bring your kids," David said.

"None of us *have* kids." Miguel opened the conference room door. "We're all married to this job. I'm not so sure if that's a good thing or just plain sad."

Nick hustled around the table, filing out behind Madeline. "Hey, are you going to be all right on this one?" he asked in a low voice, coming up beside her. "I know it hits close to home."

She'd been with BAU for five years and Nick for four. They'd worked together on several close-call cases. Nick was privy to a little more about her past and what drove her than some of the others on the team.

He used to know better than to ask her such a question.

Ever since he started dating Aubrey Flood, an ER doctor he reconnected with two months ago while trying to stop a copycat killer, he caught a severe case of feelings and started lowering his walls around everyone.

It was equal parts inviting and invasive.

Straightening her posture as she quickened her pace, Madeline pulled on a tight smile. "When have you ever known me not to be all right?" No matter how challenging, scary or gruesome things got, she didn't simply muster through. She stayed at the top of her game, always, and never let anything, personal or otherwise, stand in the way of her doing her job.

He ran a hand through his dirty blond hair.

"What we do is tough. It takes everything we have until there isn't much left at times, but we rise to meet the demands. That doesn't mean we aren't human. It's natural if a case gets to us sometimes."

Madeline appreciated the well-meaning concern, no matter how unnecessary. "I should be asking how you're doing now that you're finally in a serious relationship."

"Better than I've been in a long time since falling for Aubrey." A ghost of a smile touched his lips, but whenever he mentioned her name his eyes lit up in an unmistakable way. "I highly recommend monogamy. You should give it a try."

She shrugged as she entered her office.

Who had time for love, much less an opportunity to find it? Nick's situation was an outlier. Then there was Liam and Lorelai Parker, the administrative assistant to Director Branson. A slow-burn office romance that was about to be sealed with marital vows didn't count either.

She slipped on her navy blue windbreaker that had FBI printed across the back.

Nick grabbed his jacket from across the hall. "But I'm guessing your earlier deflection means I struck a nerve."

More like an old wound that healed a little bit each time she rescued a child, but she didn't confirm or deny his astute assessment.

"And for the record," Nick continued, "you never answered my question."

"I'm fine." She'd joined the FBI with the goal of becoming a kidnapping expert. Sure, whenever they got a case like this, it burned Madeline's gut that another innocent child had been snatched, but this was what she lived for: a chance to save a young life and spare a family an agonizing loss.

She was going to do absolutely everything in her power to bring Emma Rhodes home alive and well. No matter the personal cost.

Chapter Two

"I've already answered this question." Jackson Rhodes bit back impatience as he paced in front of the first-floor conference room. Seattle Police Department officers swarmed around the atrium, buzzing like bees in a hive, collecting statements from employees and vendors for the past hour. Still, they had nothing to go on. "Shouldn't you be trying to find my daughter instead of making me repeat myself?"

"It's important for us to go over every detail of your statement." Detective Dowd's flat, indifferent voice only ramped up Jackson's anxiety. "Make sure there are no inconsistencies."

Inconsistencies? Jackson stopped cold and glared at the detective. "What are you implying? That I might be lying about what happened?"

The detective sighed. "This is standard procedure, sir." His gaze shifted to something over Jackson's shoulder. "Finally," he muttered.

Turning, Jackson spotted the FBI team crossing the atrium. Four of them, maybe more. After exchanging a few hurried words, they each took off in a different direction. One made a beeline his way, badge hooked on her waistband on the opposite hip from where her gun was holstered.

Dowd tipped his head at the statuesque woman. "You have no idea how good it is to see you." He looked back at Jackson with relief stamped on his face. "Mr. Rhodes, this is Special Agent Madeline Striker, one of the FBI's best kidnapping experts."

Agent Striker proffered her hand. She was attractive with golden brown skin, long dark hair swept up in a low, loose chignon and a steely demeanor.

Jackson stepped forward, accepting her hand. Warm fingers wrapped around his and squeezed with surprising strength, sending an electric prickle down his spine. He quickly dropped his hand, ignoring the sensation that pulled him from his thoughts for a nanosecond.

"Mr. Rhodes, we're going to do everything in our power to get your daughter back as quickly as possible." Her confident bearing and the utter lack of pity on her face loosened the tightness in his chest.

It gave him the glimmer of hope that this nightmare might not end badly. "Thank you. Please call me Jackson."

Another woman in her midtwenties approached

them. She was younger than Agent Striker by a handful of years. Tall and slender, she greeted him with the type of worrisome expression that he was beginning to dread.

"This is my colleague, Caitlyn Yang," Agent Striker said. "She's our communications liaison."

Jackson acknowledged her with a nod.

The younger woman flashed a forced smile in return and then glanced at the detective. "Thanks for the timely updates."

"Only doing my job," Dowd said. He looked at his notepad. "I was just about to go over Mr. Rhodes's statement."

"For the second time," Jackson snapped, renewed frustration mounting inside him.

"I can't imagine how difficult this must be for you," Ms. Yang said. The compassion in her voice rubbed Jackson raw and it was almost more than he could bear. "Why don't you have a seat?" she suggested, taking his elbow and gesturing to a chair.

Jackson jerked his arm away. "I don't need to be handled." He was an expert at managing people. Reading them during a negotiation and knowing precisely how to respond. The reversal of being on the receiving end was a pointed reminder that for the first time in his life he was completely powerless.

"I was only trying to help," Yang said.

"The police have been here over an hour and

they don't have a single lead. Not one. More than a hundred people are out there and you mean to tell me that no one saw a damn thing? If you think trying to coddle me is helpful, you're mistaken."

Yang lowered her shock-filled gaze while Dowd released a heavy sigh and pursed his lips.

Jackson's heart hammered like a brutal fist against his rib cage. "I don't need to repeat my statement. You should be taking action. Questioning the vendors again. Scouring through the surveillance footage. Combing the streets to find my daughter!"

Instead of squandering precious time.

Time that should be spent searching for Emma.

He'd read that the first forty-eight hours were the most critical. The longer she was missing, the odds of finding her alive dwindled exponentially. The thought that his little girl might never come home again made his knees shake.

Jackson was hanging on by a thread, but he managed to push the weakness aside.

It wouldn't do Emma any good if he broke down. He paced in the conference room, needing space to breathe, but the suffocating sensation didn't ease.

Agent Striker gave Jackson a probing stare. Her sharp brown eyes simmered with a beguiling energy. Her unreadable expression didn't change. She didn't even blink.

He gritted his teeth at not having any inkling as to what she was thinking.

"Detective," Agent Striker said, "why don't you share his statement with Caitlyn while I take over the family support role with Mr. Rhodes."

Dowd raised a conciliatory hand. "No arguments here." The gray-haired man flicked his pad closed. He turned along with Yang and the two left the conference room.

"Mr. Rhodes, I assure you that neither I, nor any law enforcement officer here, have any intention of wasting your time since we have none to spare," Agent Striker said matter-of-factly, as if reading his thoughts. "I understand the inquiry process can feel tedious, frustrating even, but it's necessary." Grim resolve settled across her face. "Our only goal is to find your daughter, and I give you my word, I'll do everything possible."

The statement broke through the haze of his panic, steadying him. This was what he needed. A solid professional unencumbered by sentimentality running the case.

"All right." He took a deep breath. "I'm sorry for raising my voice and trying to tell everyone how to do their job." That was so unlike him. Not the part about issuing orders or giving constructive criticism, but losing his temper. He could be brusque at times. Never rude. "To be honest, I'm angry at myself. Emma wanted to go somewhere to see a puppy. She even asked permission the way I'd taught her." Like a good girl following the rules. "I was distracted, told her to wait. Then the next thing I knew she was gone." Vanished without a trace. "Turns out there wasn't any puppy on the premises."

"Kidnappers often entice and lure children away with the prospect of something that's hard to resist, like going somewhere fun. Getting candy. Petting a puppy."

"The nanny had offered to come. Had said it wouldn't be any trouble. If only I hadn't given Liane the day off."

"Her last name?"

"Strothe. With an e at the end."

Madeline withdrew a smartphone from her pocket and began typing. "How long has she been with you?"

"A little less than two years. Why? You don't think Liane had anything to do with this, do you?"

"Why didn't you want her to come?"

"Emma was going to be with me the entire day." He had promised her no work under any circumstances. "I had arranged to leave early because I wanted to take her to the Space Needle, for a ride on the monorail and treat her to ice cream." They had spent a week planning what they were going to do together. "I relish the time I have with her. Liane never takes personal days, and I didn't see any reason to waste her free time." All true, but there was a deeper, underlying truth he couldn't admit out loud. On Family Day, everyone brought their kids and spouse. Not their nanny. People at ETC already thought him an elitist snob. He hadn't wanted to perpetuate the distorted perception. "Worst-case scenario, I knew I could rely on my assistant, Brittany, to help me out, but I was foolish not to bring Liane. This might never have happened if I had."

Damn trying to repair his image.

"This isn't your fault, Mr. Rhodes."

Maybe not, but it didn't lighten the crushing weight of guilt bearing down on him. Or the simple fact that if he had paid closer attention to Emma, she'd be in his arms right now. Not missing. "It's Jackson. Please."

This federal agent was his best chance at getting back the most important person in the world to him. Fostering some familiarity couldn't hurt. It might even prove beneficial.

"Call me Madeline."

"Is Liane a suspect? I got her through a highly respected agency I've used for a long time. They do background checks, drug testing, the works."

"We'll need to question everyone who has had close contact with your daughter before we can rule them out. The nanny. Your assistant. Do you have a housekeeper? Personal chef? A driver?"

"Time is my most valuable resource, but I don't have that kind of household staff." He never fit in with the jet-setting, country-clubbing one percent who did. But he wanted to make sure his daughter felt at ease around anyone, whether it was in a soup kitchen or on a yacht. "I have Liane to help, I use a cleaning service and I have groceries delivered. I do the cooking for Emma and myself unless we eat out. As much as possible, I prefer to be hands-on."

Madeline raised an eyebrow. "Considering you're a single parent with a high-pressure position at ETC and the means to hire a personal staff, that's commendable."

To him, it was the least his daughter deserved. "How will you figure out who took Emma?"

"We'll look at the evidence, compile a list of suspects and run everything to the ground," she said. "Do you have any enemies?"

"No."

Madeline's eyes narrowed as though the response had been delivered too fast. Or she suspected it had been a lie. Her cell phone pinged, and she read her text message. "You were recently named CEO, a position that comes with a lot of power, money and prestige. I'm sure you didn't achieve that without ruffling a few feathers."

"You're right. I didn't get this job by trying to win a popularity contest, but you're asking if I ruffled feathers to the point someone would want to kidnap my daughter."

Her gaze settled hard on him. "Yes."

Success had required making tough choices. He had bruised egos and hurt feelings during his climb up the ladder. All for the sake of business. Nothing personal, and he had always treated everyone fairly. It wasn't as if he was a monster. "No. There's no one."

Doubt rocked through him. *Someone* had taken Emma. For every action, there was a reaction. Basic physics.

The chasm of guilt inside him deepened.

"Have you had a bad breakup recently, say within the last six months? Ended a relationship when the other person wasn't ready to say goodbye?" Madeline asked.

Jackson scoffed. "No relationships. No dalliances. No breakups. Not even a one-night stand." His love life had been one big black hole for four years, much less the past six months.

"Who stands the most to gain from your resignation?"

The most obvious implication hadn't occurred to him. "The vice president. Andrew Phillips. He's next in line. Always wanted the job."

Madeline typed on her smartphone, again.

"Excuse me, but may I ask what's so important on your phone?"

"I'm checking red alerts from the team, any potential suspects they come up with, and inputting what I learn in a shared document. The process is efficient and timely, but I'm still focused on everything you say." She looked up at him. "Please continue."

"Andrew would be the one to fill in for me. At least temporarily, until the board officially designates my replacement." Andrew had been there at the start of Family Day. When was the last time anyone had seen him?

Jackson spun toward the atrium and scanned the crowd, looking for him.

Madeline glanced in the same direction, then caught his eye. "The kidnapper contacted you via text?"

"Yes." Jackson nodded, recalling how terrifying it had been to receive the demand, the acknowledgment that Emma had been taken, but it had also been a relief. He had something to act on. A reason to hope there was a chance to get his daughter back. "Don't kidnappers usually issue ransom demands through a phone call?"

"Most times, but not always. We'll need your cell phone to trace the text."

"My IT person, Rivka Molnar, is cracking away at that as we speak. She's one of the best there is in the business." As soon as Rivka had given her statement to the police and dropped her own daughter off at school, she'd gotten to work on it.

"No doubt. Nevertheless, we'll need to have our people take a look."

"Of course." Surely the FBI had their own protocol and needed to verify everything.

Another ping on Madeline's phone drew her attention to the screen. "Where can we find Ms. Molnar?"

"This floor. In a restricted area, beyond security. You need a badge to access it."

With a nod, she began typing. "Apparently, our techie, Liam McDare, is in security now, reviewing the surveillance footage. He'll take care of it."

"I suppose I should contact the media, set up a press conference so I can resign publicly per the demands." The sooner he did so, the sooner he might get his daughter back.

"I'd advise against that." Madeline lowered her phone. "I don't think it's a good idea."

His heart twisted into a knot. "Why? It was the one thing the kidnapper demanded." The only thing. Not money. Not power. "My resignation in exchange for Emma's safe return."

She opened her mouth to respond, but Rivka darted past two police officers into the conference room.

"Jackson!" Rivka rushed to him with his cell phone in her hand.

"Agent Striker—Madeline—this is Rivka Molnar. The head of the IT department I was telling you about."

"I traced the number," Rivka said, cheeks flushed, stray red curls that had escaped her ponytail hanging around her face. She handed him the phone. "It was easier than I expected considering the circumstances. Almost too easy, now that I think about it."

"I won't look a gift horse in the mouth." Riding a fresh surge of adrenaline, Jackson stepped closer. "What's the location where the text was sent from?"

"Believe it or not, one of our remote work sites. Off I-99 across from the Duwamish Waterway."

"What?" Jackson shook his head. "That doesn't make any sense."

"I agree, it is strange. I cloned your phone for the FBI. They have all the metadata and can monitor any further communication in real time. Liam McDare is going to have an Agent West verify the trace."

"If Ms. Molnar missed anything," Madeline said, "I have every confidence that between West and McDare they'll find it. What's the exact address of the work site?"

Questions whirled in Jackson's mind and there was only one way to get answers. "I'm heading over there." He started toward the atrium. "It's less than ten minutes away. You can follow me or ride along. But don't think of suggesting that I stay behind. Not when the text originated from ETC property and it looks as if it might've been an employee who has taken Emma." The thought of such a betrayal burned his gut. "I have to go. That's nonnegotiable."

Madeline hurried ahead of him, bringing him to a quick stop with a raised palm. "No one can force you to stay here, but riding *with us* would be faster," she said in a firm, impassive voice that he found oddly soothing. "You'll have to stay in the vehicle while we check the facility and question employees. That's also nonnegotiable. Can you do that, Jackson?"

He would do whatever was necessary to get his little girl back. Emma was his true north, his whole world. Without question, he would make any sacrifice to protect her. Lay down his own life in a heartbeat. Truth be told, if it came down to it, he would take a life, too. "I can."

Madeline led the way through the atrium toward two FBI agents who were questioning the chairman and Jackson's assistant, Brittany, separately. A succession of pings had all three agents glancing at their phones.

Both agents broke off their interviews and approached Madeline.

"Jackson Rhodes, this is Supervisory Special Agent Miguel Peters," Madeline said, gesturing to a man with dark hair, "and Special Agent Nick James." She indicated the other somber-looking agent as perfunctory handshakes were exchanged. "Jackson would prefer us to dispense with the formality of titles and surnames."

"We just got the update on the location of the trace from Liam," Miguel said to Madeline. "I'll stay with Dash and handle things here, finish collecting statements and reviewing the surveillance footage." He handed her car keys.

Nick's gaze shifted to Madeline. "I'll go with you."

Miguel nodded. "Take Caitlyn as well and a few of the police officers standing around."

"Jackson is also going to come," Madeline said. "It might be useful to have him on-site."

Miguel glanced at Jackson and looked him over a moment, then he turned back to Madeline. "If you think it's best for him to go along, I won't question it."

Jackson and Madeline made their way outside the front of the building while Nick rounded up the others. Madeline climbed in behind the wheel of one of the two black SUVs that were parked near squad cars. He slid into the front passenger seat beside her.

She cranked the engine and entered the address he rattled off into the GPS.

The second Nick and Caitlyn hopped in the back of the vehicle, Madeline peeled out of the spot.

With blue-and-red lights flashing on the dash and the sirens blaring on the police cruisers that followed them, Madeline wove through traffic at a speed that had Jackson clutching the armrest.

In this situation, there was no such thing as too fast. He was relieved Madeline acted as such.

"Why do you have a remote site?" Madeline asked.

"It's not uncommon. We have several for different reasons. Sometimes the issue is space. Out at the Duwamish site, it's for secrecy. Top-of-the-line security. The facility has metal detectors, and no one can even bring a cell phone inside. Everyone who works there has been through the most stringent of background checks."

Madeline's gaze flickered to him. "What is ETC working on?"

Years of secrecy caused Jackson to hesitate. Under normal circumstances, a civilian would have to sign a nondisclosure agreement before he answered the question. Nothing about today was normal. "Cloaking technology. The team is finishing a prototype. We're hoping to get a government contract."

"With DARPA?" Caitlyn asked, referring to the Defense Advanced Research Projects Agency.

"Yes. They deal with all the breakthrough technology for national security. We're talking the potential for billions in profit." Jackson had fought to expand the company, take ETC in a bold, innovative direction. Against all odds, he had scraped together the money to save the company from the brink of bankruptcy while funding the venture. "It's my pet project. Sort of my..."

He swallowed hard, nearly choking on the words sticking in his throat.

Caitlyn and Nick stared at Jackson in the rear-view mirror.

"Your what?" Madeline asked.

"Everyone at the office jokes that it's…my baby. My second child." A cold finger ran across his heart.

Jackson clenched his hand and leaned back against the seat. He didn't know exactly what it meant that the text had been traced to that specific location, but there was no doubt in his mind that it held horrible significance.

"Are visitors allowed inside the remote site?" Nick asked. "For deliveries? Repairs? Standard maintenance?"

Jackson looked back over the seat. "No, we have strict protocols in place. Only cleared personnel. Anyone who steps foot inside the facility has been thoroughly vetted."

"We need to know all the employees who have access to the Duwamish site," Madeline said. "See if any had a grievance or might be vulnerable to blackmail."

"I'll call Dash," Caitlyn said, taking out her phone. She dialed and relayed the message, then listened. "Okay. Thanks." She disconnected. "They verified the trace. The text did originate from that location. Dash said there was no attempt to mask the trail. Also, the surveillance footage inside ETC headquarters was on a loop. That's why there's no coverage of who took Emma."

Something about this was wrong. The details didn't add up. "The kidnapper was savvy enough to put our surveillance feed on a loop, but not cover their tracks of the text message?" Jackson asked.

No one said a word. They didn't have to. The cagey looks from the others told Jackson all he needed to know. They were thinking the same thing.

Almost too easy. Rivka's words came back in a rush, filling him with foreboding.

Madeline exited I-99 and took Alaskan Way to East Marginal. Once they made a right toward the work site, the gated facility was visible.

Alarm crept over him.

Employees were gathered outside the building in the parking lot. Twenty of them, which accounted for the entire team plus security, stood about a hundred feet from the building near the fence line.

"What in the hell?" Nick muttered.

Madeline and Jackson traded wary glances as she stopped at the entrance and rolled down the window.

Jackson leaned over and waved to the security guard. "What's going on?"

"Mr. Rhodes." The guard's eyebrows rose in

surprise. "The carbon monoxide alarms went off in the building. Everyone had to evacuate. I called the fire department and gas company. The SFD should be here any minute."

Almost too easy. Now a carbon monoxide leak?

Jackson stiffened. "What if Emma is inside?" The stray thought struck him as irrational. The odds of his little girl being in there, without anyone noticing, were as slim as someone who worked at the site being the culprit. But the events of the day had already taught him anything was possible.

"Is this the only way in and out?" Madeline asked Jackson.

"Yes. Single point of entry for added security."

Her gaze swung back to the guard. "Has anyone entered or left the premises in the past hour?"

"No, ma'am," the guard said.

The news kept Jackson from doing something rash, like leaping from the vehicle and racing inside the building against Madeline's instructions, though it wasn't nearly enough to bring him a shred of relief.

"The funny thing is," the guard added, "there's a strange smell in the building."

"But carbon monoxide is odorless," Madeline said.

"That's what makes it so weird."

"Think this is some kind of a diversion?" Nick

asked. "A slew of uncleared people are about to circumvent protocol and get access in there."

"It's possible," Madeline said. "We shouldn't rule anything out." She looked back at the guard. "Make sure no one leaves the premises unless they've been cleared by the FBI or the police."

"You've got it." The armed guard buzzed them in. A second later, the heavy gate rolled opened.

They drove past the gaggle of employees, closer to the one-story building, and parked. The state-of-the-art facility was small. The east side of it was comprised of a meditation room, break room with a kitchen, gym and locker room since the team spent long days hard at work. The other half of the building—which faced the Duwamish Waterway, giving the team a western view and natural light through the privacy-tinted wall of windows—was entirely for research and development.

"Sit tight and let us handle this," Madeline said.

Jackson nodded in reluctant agreement.

The others jumped out of the vehicle and huddled up by the open trunk.

Madeline and Nick took off their jackets and strapped on bulletproof vests while she doled out orders. "Caitlyn, have the officers help you collect statements from everyone. We'll do a sweep inside to make sure there's no one left."

The communications liaison and the uniformed officers headed to the cluster of ETC employees.

Nick and Madeline both drew their weapons. As they advanced toward the building, Jackson hopped out of the SUV.

Pulse hammering, he edged forward, desperate for definitive proof as to who had taken his daughter. But he stopped, fighting against the overwhelming urge. Better to leave this part to law enforcement. Though nothing, other than finding Emma unharmed, would make this better.

Tension coiled through him, what-ifs stacking up in his mind. What if whoever had sent the text was no longer here? Or what if the trace was a dead end?

Madeline and Nick were side by side, their guns raised.

Watching the Feds draw closer, Jackson scrubbed a hand over his jaw. His heartbeat pounded in his ears. He ached to do something, other than wait, but at the same time, he couldn't shake the sense that something about this was wrong—really, really wrong.

The two agents got within ten paces of the front door. And then…

The west side of the building exploded.

Chapter Three

Madeline and Nick staggered to a halt as a blaze consumed the interior of the building's west side. Heat surged from the broken windows, exploding the remaining panes, but her blood chilled.

If the timing had been different—two minutes, maybe less—they would've both been inside. She risked her life on a regular basis—that came with the territory. But this had been a close call.

Too close.

Fire licked the air through the shattered opening. Gray smoke billowed out across the water.

Madeline looked over her shoulder.

Jackson stood aghast, gaping at the building. At the ruins of his pet project. His baby.

Madeline holstered her weapon and went to him.

His eyes were glassy with horror. His skin, his coloring was too pale. The same paralyzing fear she'd seen on countless other parents rolled off him in waves.

She put a hand on his shoulder. "The fire department will be here shortly. They'll search the building and confirm if it was empty."

For a long moment, she wondered if he'd heard her. Even Nick gave her a concerned glance that had her regretting the fact that she'd allowed Jackson to come along.

"Thank you," Jackson said in a low voice, still staring at the fire.

She let out a small breath of relief that he'd spoken. "For what?"

Finally, his gaze met hers. "Not asking me if I'm all right."

It was obvious he wasn't. In a few short hours, everything that mattered most to him had been taken away. This man was suffering from a pain beyond what the physical could inflict and it was etched all over his face.

"You said that you don't have any enemies, but..." Madeline took a second, needing to find the right words. "This was well-timed. Meticulously executed. I need you to think hard about who might want to target you in this way."

He stepped back, shrugging off her hand. "If I knew something that could be useful, anything that might help me get my daughter back, don't you think I'd tell you in a heartbeat? I have no idea who did this." He threw a hand up at the building. "No idea why."

The kidnapper hadn't asked for ransom money.

Only his resignation. Which meant that Jackson did know who was responsible. He just couldn't see it yet.

"What about Andrew Phillips?" Nick asked. "Your assistant told me that in the event you step down, he'd be the one to fill in for you. Or how about Charles Albrecht, the CEO of Albrech-Tech? I overheard the chairman mention that you two have a combative rivalry."

"That's true. There's been infighting between me and Andrew since day one. And as for Chuck, *combative* is putting it mildly." Jackson's cheeks turned a mottled shade of red. "But to think that either of them would go to such lengths…" He glanced at the fiery ruins of his project. "It's un-imaginable."

Nick rocked back on his heels and peered up at the sky. "Well, what do we have here?"

Madeline followed the direction he pointed in, spotting the whirring device at once. A small quadcopter drone fitted with a camera hovered above the parking lot.

How long had it been there?

She couldn't hear the rotor blades due to the roar of the fire, but if the drone had been over-head when they stepped out of the vehicle, she would've noticed the noise.

"We're being watched." Nick hiked his chin up.

"By the person who kidnapped Emma?" Jackson asked.

"Safe assumption," Madeline said. Her gut told her any other explanation would be too much of a coincidence, and she didn't believe in those.

"Why use a drone?" Jackson asked. "Did the sick bastard want to watch the explosion?" He glared up at the quadcopter, fists at his sides. "I'll give you whatever you want! Just release my little girl! Please. Let Emma go."

"They're usually only equipped with video, no audio," Nick said.

Dropping his head, Jackson slapped the hood of the SUV and muttered a curse.

Madeline got the sense he was a man used to being in total and complete control, of himself, of everything in his orbit. Even now, looking on the verge of falling apart, he was working hard to hold it together.

She turned to Nick. "See if you can shoot the drone down." It was within range and Nick was a good shot. "We might get lucky. Pull a set of prints." Everyone made mistakes sooner or later. Maybe the kidnapper got sloppy, hadn't considered this possibility. If so, they could use it to their advantage.

"Sure."

While Nick quickly took aim, Madeline opened the front passenger door and ushered Jackson inside the vehicle. Fortunately, he sat without a fight. Giving whoever was watching the video more footage of Jackson unraveling wouldn't help the situation. If anything, it'd only feed the perpetrator's ego.

Madeline stayed between the door and the frame.

A pair of gunshots rang out, making Jackson flinch. She was used to the sharp sound, but the loud report always came as a surprise to most civilians.

Nick had managed to drop the quadcopter to the ground on the second shot. He grabbed an evidence bag from the trunk and tugged on gloves before retrieving it.

"I know commercial drones aren't equipped with audio." Jackson loosened his tie and pulled it off over his head. His tailored suit did nothing to hide the bulk of his muscles or the unbearable weight he was carrying. "If it were, at two hundred feet high, it'd capture very little audio from the ground. Factor in prop noise and it'd be useless." His shoulders slumped forward, his brow creasing as a hand jerked the top button on his collar open. "No point in screaming at it the way I did. Like an idiot. I think I'm in shock from it all."

There was something in his voice, a deep, dark underlying sadness that caught her breath. That made her soften in a way she hadn't for a long time.

The desire to comfort him was startling in its intensity. She clenched her hand to keep from touching him. The rest of the BAU team thought the impact on the parents was never her concern, but they couldn't have been more wrong. The reason she kept her distance from the victims' loved ones, normally letting Caitlyn handle the support role instead, was that she understood their suffering all too well. The closer she got to the family, the easier it was to get caught in the emotional undertow. Then how would she be able to save the victim?

She swallowed to clear her throat. "What you're feeling is only natural. To be expected."

Sirens wailed in the distance. It was convenient the fire department had already been called and was on the way. They might be able to get the blaze under control quickly.

"Did he hit the drone?" Jackson asked.

"Yes." She gave an encouraging nod. Any glimmer of hope she could offer she would gladly give. Not only for Jackson's sake, but for her own as well. Far too many kidnapping cases, like the one involving her sister, didn't have a happy ending. The families were left devastated. Broken. Sometimes beyond repair. She shook herself, refusing to let ugly memories distract her. "It's pretty much intact. We'll have it dusted."

She glanced back at Nick, who was sealing the evidence bag.

Movement in the sky snatched her gaze. Another drone was following, and a second. *Oh, no.*

Whoever planned this had indeed taken into consideration the prospect of losing one. Slim odds they'd find any prints. There went a possible lead.

Her heart sank.

"What is it now?" Jackson asked.

Madeline chided herself for reacting and wiped the expression from her face which had given away that something else was wrong. "More drones."

The sirens grew louder from the approaching fire trucks.

Jackson's phone chimed. He fished his cell from his inner jacket pocket.

"Another text, from an unknown number." He swiped the screen and read the message out loud.

"Behold the demonstration of my resolve. Appreciate the mercy shown to your employees. Understand the FBI can't help you. Resign on camera when the press arrives. Fail and your daughter pays the ultimate price."

Unease twisted Madeline's stomach into a knot. The carbon monoxide alarm had been deliberately triggered. This was all a ploy to evacuate the building and spare the workers' lives. "Let me see it." After reading it once, she'd have the text committed to memory.

Jackson handed it over. "I bet this time it won't be traceable."

She was inclined to agree, but she knew better than to voice the concern. "Our team will still try everything possible."

"What won't be traceable?" Nick set the bagged drone down in the trunk.

"Second text message," Madeline said. "Further demands."

Nick closed the door and came around the side of the vehicle. She passed him the cell phone.

Two fire trucks pulled through the gate as Nick read the message. "Another doozy. Let's see if the number will receive a text." He thumbed a few quick words. A second later, he shook his head. "Message delivery failed. One-way communication."

Jackson buttoned his collar, put his tie on and adjusted it.

"What are you doing?" Madeline asked.

"Preparing to go on camera." He combed back his blond hair with his fingers, not leaving a strand out of place. Within seconds, he appeared polished and poised. "Resign like the kidnapper wants. The press will be here any minute."

There was no doubt in Madeline's mind that every local news station had received an anonymous tip about the explosion, ensuring full press coverage would be imminent.

As if on cue, a KIRO 7 *Eyewitness News* chopper zipped through the sky, taking a position over the water with a prime vantage point of the blazing inferno.

The kidnapper was smart and miles ahead of them, tightening their control of the situation at a brutal pace. Madeline had to change the dynamic, shift the balance of power somehow and buy them time, even just a little. "You can't resign. It's the only card you have to play."

"Can't?" Jackson's eyes narrowed, growing cold. He got out of the SUV, towering over her and sucking up the air with his fury.

Madeline stood her ground. Jackson was a distraught parent. Terrified. Angry. Frantic. Although the whirlwind of emotion raging inside him was directed at her, it wasn't because of her. "You *shouldn't* resign. It's not the right play."

"I don't have a choice." He pushed past her and Nick.

"Please listen to me." She kept her voice calm and firm despite the panic welling in her gut. "I do think you should go on camera."

Jackson stopped and turned. "And say what?"

"Demand proof of life. A video of Emma telling you something only she would know. Maybe the name of her favorite toy. Footage could reveal clues to help us find her, and the kidnapper won't expect it." There were no guarantees, but she was fairly certain Jackson issuing a demand would throw the unsub—unknown subject—

off-kilter. Emma's captor wanted to avoid direct confrontation and expected everyone to play by their rules. Perhaps that's why the demands were sent via text. A phone call invited discussion, negotiation. A one-way text left no opportunity for debate.

"Which also means not doing as I was told might antagonize him," Jackson said. "Provoke the psycho to lash out. Retaliate."

A point she couldn't deny. "I'm well aware of the risks. But this is worth taking the chance. Her abductor, whoever it is, has thought this out. He's prepared. Even worse, he's changed the terms as he sees fit, according to his timetable. First you had twenty-four hours to resign and now you've got, what? Twenty minutes before there are camera crews out front. We need time to catch up. I'm right about this." She was sure of it.

"I don't know," Jackson shook his head. "Sounds too risky."

"You should listen to her," Nick said. "She's the best kidnapping expert I've ever seen. She knows how to handle an unsub. If anyone can get Emma back with the least possible risk, it's Madeline. You need to trust her judgment."

Jackson's steely gaze bounced between them before settling on her a beat. He stroked a hand over his mouth, the troubled expression on his face not fading. He was assessing her, deliberating. His silence signified he didn't trust her. Not that she would let that rattle her.

Faith in self was essential in this business. She needed the unshakable kind that would get Emma home safely.

Given the chance, her plan would work and prove to Jackson that he could rely on her expertise. But if it backfired, she could have an emotional parent going rogue to contend with.

She had to convince him. "The kidnapper made sure to evacuate the building and detonate the bomb before we went inside," Madeline said, closing the gap between them. "This person doesn't want the situation to escalate to murder. When you're on camera, talk about Emma, use her name a lot. You have to humanize her to her abductor."

"I'll need my phone back," Jackson said. "To show the press a few pictures."

"Good idea." Madeline gestured to Nick and he gave the phone to Jackson. "Remember, winning a negotiation requires patience and keeping our heads. But whatever you do, don't resign. Not yet. As grim as it might sound, we need to know that Emma is alive. Then and only then should you comply with the demand."

GUILT THRUMMED THROUGH Jackson faster and hotter than the blood in his veins as he stood in front of a gaggle of reporters. Cameras and mics were pointed at him. Everyone waited for him to make a statement after the communications liaison, Caitlyn, had explained the circumstances regarding the kidnapping and the explosion.

Everything was on the line. Emma's life. His own life because he wouldn't survive losing his only child.

It was his fault she had been taken in the first place. He'd let down his guard, looked away for a moment too long, brushed aside his daughter's eagerness to see a puppy.

No more mistakes.

"I appreciate the assistance from local law enforcement and the FBI." Jackson swallowed in an attempt to clear the emotion thickening his throat. "I'd like to address the person holding my daughter captive. Whoever you are, I beg you not to hurt Emma." He held up a picture of her on his cell phone, giving the cameramen an opportunity to zoom in on the photo of her taken this morning, posing in her pantsuit, before he swiped to the next one of her. "She gets cold easily and is allergic to strawberries. She's a sweet, loving child. Creative. Spirited. Kind. She has the biggest heart."

A favorite image of Emma—curly blond halo of hair and her face lighting up when he had surprised her with her first horseback riding lesson, the way she threw her arms around his neck and squeezed—rose in his mind like an apparition.

Pure joy bled into stark fear.

Proof of life.

Madeline was right. He needed to know his daughter was still alive, but at what cost?

The kidnapper had been startlingly persuasive with that fiery demonstration. Someone who was willing to kidnap an innocent child and blow up a building was capable of anything.

More images flooded him, holidays, birthdays, breakfasts, bedtime. He struggled to stem the tide.

Fail and your daughter pays the ultimate price.

His mind spun, but tremors erupted in his heart. They spread down his arms, tingling in his fingers. The phone shook in his hand.

No matter what happened to him, he only wanted Emma to be safe. To grow up and live a long, happy life. No sacrifice on his part was too great.

"Per your demands, I hereby resign as CEO from ETC effective immediately. But I need to know that my daughter is okay. That you haven't hurt her. I need to see her, do you understand? Send me a video of Emma showing that she hasn't been harmed and in it have her tell you what she wished for on her last birthday. Once you do, ETC will release a press statement confirming that my resignation is officially binding and permanent."

Jackson turned his back on the press and

stalked away from the flurry of questions the press hurled at him and made his way back through the Duwamish gate.

The fire was being contained. Gray smoke filled the sky above the building. Nick was busy coordinating with the fire department while Madeline was on an intercept course with Jackson.

He kept walking toward the SUV.

Though he could no longer see her behind him, he was aware that she was hot on his heels.

"What was that?" Madeline asked once they were out of earshot of the press and employees.

He stopped and faced her. "I'm sure you're good at your job. Hell, you might even be the best, but I haven't vetted you. I don't know your track record, if there are any red flags, what's your success-to-failure ratio, the number of hostages who haven't been rescued. The only thing I know for certain is that every instinct I have is screaming that compliance was the right call. And I always trust my gut."

"I can understand that. Respect it even. I always trust mine as well. But vetted or not, I am an expert for a reason. I've been through this many times. What you did was in direct opposition of the play I advised."

"With all due respect, this isn't a game. You may be a kidnapping expert, but the one thing I specialize in is risk assessment. This is my daughter we're talking about here, and it was too risky to antagonize the person who has her. I will not take unnecessary chances when it comes to Emma."

"Kidnapping situations can go wrong. There have been casualties in my previous cases, but none of them a victim. I have never lost someone."

"Not yet." No one had a perfect record forever.

She drew herself up, standing taller, and stared him dead in the eye. "I don't intend to let Emma be my first."

"Do you have children, Madeline?"

A flicker of emotion slashed across her face before she tensed and staggered back a step as though the question had been a physical blow. Then she went completely still. "No." All the strength that had been in her voice a moment ago was gone. "I don't."

"Then you can't possibly understand my position. For all your effort and good intentions, you and the rest of the FBI will walk away from this case once it's done and move on to the next. But this is my life. And this was my choice to make. One only I have to live with." Strip away the credentials, the experience, sense of duty, and this boiled down to something far more organic. A parent's love. "I will not, under any circumstances, gamble with my daughter's life."

Chapter Four

"I can't believe he went rogue, on television, to the press," Madeline said, standing in the smaller, more personal conference room at BAU headquarters. She clenched the back of a chair, letting her fingers dig into the leather. "I thought we had an understanding."

She had hoped she'd convinced Jackson Rhodes to trust her professional expertise. To work with her and follow her instructions.

It was a good thing Caitlyn had taken over with him to oversee the setup of the tap on his home landline and personal computer while the rest of the team regrouped. If she was standing in front of him right now, what she had to say to him might not reflect the most diplomatic choice of words.

Miguel swallowed a bite of his sandwich from Emerald City Roasters and wiped his mouth. "The situation could've been worse. At least he asked for proof of life," he said, and she agreed, but the situation could have been better, leaving them in a stronger position. "Don't beat yourself up over this. It happens to the best of us."

"Not to me. Not on my watch." An emotional parent going rogue could jeopardize this case just as much as her getting the profile of an unsub wrong. That's why she always took her time, analyzed every angle and relied on her training to help her connect the dots. Sometimes in the field a split-second decision had to be made, but only rookies made a rash call.

"First time for everything." Dash leaned back in his chair with a smug look and folded his arms.

How could Jackson be so...

She wasn't sure what he was. Reckless. Infuriating. Good-looking to the point of distraction. A wild card.

A parent acting out of conviction. And love. Madeline's heart softened a little more as her temperature cooled.

There was no denying that giving in to the demands against her advice took a great deal of courage, even if it had made her job harder.

With a shake of her head, she suppressed her reluctant admiration, yanked out a chair and sat. "Where do we stand on statements from those who were there?"

"I prioritized the catering crew of three, the magician and the band," Dash said. "Every year, ETC uses the same catering company, but their staff has a high turnover rate. A lot of college kids who need part-time employment. No one working on the crew that day knew each other. I ran checks on them but turned up nothing. They were all clean. Same with the magician and band. Everyone was so busy doing their job, they didn't notice anything."

"We still have hundreds of statements left to review." David munched on fries from his to-go container. "The cops didn't flag anything as suspicious. No one saw a young girl being led away. It'll take me a couple of days to go through them all, compare for discrepancies. Honestly, it's going to be a nightmare of busywork. I know that's what us interns are here for, but the kidnapper picked the worst possible day."

"Actually, the kidnapper picked the perfect day." Madeline sipped her coffee, still wound too tight to stomach any food, despite the tempting aromas in the air. "We're going to be stretched thin with a mountain of statements to comb through. I bet most of them will be meaningless. Tracking down anything useful will be like trying to find a needle in a haystack."

David sighed. "Great. I'm looking forward to it."

"You won't be alone." Nick clasped his shoulder. "I'll be digging in the weeds right along with you." He turned to everyone else. "Forensics is dusting the drone I shot down for prints, but I wouldn't hold my breath that they'll find anything. I jotted down the model number and looked it up. It's commercial. A popular brand called ABC Icarus. According to the specs, the drone's max speed is fifty miles per hour, and it can fly for up to thirty minutes. Whoever was operating it was within a twenty-five-mile radius."

Madeline perked in her seat at the small nugget of useful information. "That means Emma wasn't far when the building exploded. The kidnapper wouldn't have a chance to drive her out of state and return in time to maintain a visual of the Duwamish site once the ransom demand was sent. The child might've even been in the metropolitan area. Definitely within a thirty-to-forty-five-minute drive. Hopefully, she's still close by."

"What were the fire department's preliminary findings about the bomb?" Miguel asked.

"Another drone was used to deliver what appears to be a homemade explosive device along with an accelerant," Nick said. "The drone entered through the ventilation shaft on the roof. They also found soiled cat litter in the air vent, which they believe triggered the carbon monoxide alarm."

"That would explain the strange smell the employees mentioned," Madeline added. "Since the kidnapper used drones to trigger the alarms, deliver the bomb and monitor the situation, how did the text message originate from the building?"

"The text was traced to the vicinity of the Duwamish site," Dash said. "Not necessarily the building. The cell phone was detected within a small radius of three different cell towers. The area where each tower overlapped is where it was pinpointed. The person could've sent the text half a block away from the building without ever needing to go inside." His brows drew together as if he was thinking of something. "Traffic cam footage around ETC didn't turn up anything viable, but we might have better luck around the Duwamish site." Dash made himself a note.

"We have statements from the employees there," Madeline said. Each one of them seemed heartbroken over the loss of their project. All their hard work on a prototype down the drain. "I don't think any of them were involved."

"I have to agree," Nick said. "They were pretty shaken up. Even more rattled when they each learned that Rhodes's daughter had been kidnapped."

"Any clarity on the profile of our unsub?" Miguel asked her.

"After the bombing, I got the feeling that this goes deeper than business." The unsub's motives were becoming clearer. This was all about Jackson. "It's definitely a personal grudge. Someone who not only wants to hurt Jackson but also manipulate him." But to what ultimate end? She wasn't so sure this was only about him resigning anymore. "There's still something about the text messages as the form of communication that bugs me. It's one-way and doesn't give Jackson a chance to barter. This person wants Jackson to suffer, yet they haven't exploited the opportunity to hear him beg over the phone."

"Whoever it is saw him plead on TV," David said.

Nick nodded. "And he screamed at the camera on the drone. I'm sure that made for lovely footage someone could watch and revel in over and over again."

"The televised speech was tempered," Madeline said. "The drone didn't provide audio. Neither showcased his suffering. More importantly, the kidnapper hasn't bragged."

"'Behold the demonstration of my resolve,'" Dash said, reading the first line of the transcript from the last text sent by the kidnapper.

"*Resolve*. Not power. That's not boasting." Sitting forward, Madeline rested her forearms on the table. "That was persuasion. Someone doing their best to convince Jackson what kind of devastation they're capable of inflicting, but without actually hurting anyone by having the building evacuated and using three drones to ensure no one went back inside. Three. Quite clever." She drummed her fingers on the table. "The passive form of communication, the great care with the specific wording in the texts, using the promise of a puppy as the lure, not boasting—instead seeking validation. My gut tells me it's a woman. Not a man. Caucasian. Educated. Midtwenties to midthirties. I wish I could say I was a hundred percent on that, but not yet."

"Why not?" Miguel's gaze narrowed, and she stiffened under the tangible weight of his scrutiny. "What's holding you back?"

"Two things. First, I don't know why the kidnapper wanted Jackson to resign. Second, who are our top suspects?"

"Andrew Phillips and Charles Albrecht," Dash said.

Madeline nodded. "Exactly. Both men." Regardless, she couldn't shake that gut feeling, which had never led her astray. Then again, maybe Dash was right and there was a first time for everything. This could be the first time her instincts were wrong. Too many elements about this case were throwing her off. The texts. The unusual ransom demand. The wild card father with those piercing blue eyes. But when all else failed, the one thing she could rely on was her training. "We need to check the nanny and Jackson's assistant." Rivka Molnar also fit the profile. "The IT supervisor, too."

"I spoke to Ms. Molnar in depth," Dash said. "She was with her own nine-year-old when

Emma was taken. She didn't leave the premises until after the police arrived and it was to take her kid to school. Then she came straight back. We also have a brief statement from Brittany Hall, the assistant. Sounds like she was either doing something with the catering staff, the magician or the band at the time. But I went ahead and ran preliminary background checks on both as well as the nanny. No red flags."

Doubt churned through Madeline. What if she was wrong? Or she was off track with the kidnapper's profile?

Whittling down the list of suspects was a good thing, not bad, she reminded herself.

"We're looking at too many people right now for me to run a more extensive background check on everyone," Dash said.

"I did call the nanny like you wanted." David closed his food container. "Liane Strothe is coming in tomorrow."

"Thanks," Madeline said.

"Also, I noticed there wasn't a statement from Phillips. Should I schedule interviews for him and Albrecht?" David asked.

"There were numerous reports of no one seeing Phillips around the time Emma was taken," Miguel said. "He wasn't at ETC headquarters when we arrived. According to his administrative assistant, Natascha Campbell, she was with him all day up until the time he departed for Spokane for a meeting to acquire a smaller company."

"His assistant is his alibi?" Nick asked. "Do you buy her story?"

Miguel shrugged. "I'm not sure. She was a little too cagey. A gatekeeper of the first order. Fiercely loyal to Phillips, very protective. But the chairman confirmed the meeting in Spokane has been on the books for weeks. Phillips will be back tomorrow and available for an interview. With his lawyer. I'm going to speak to him first thing in the morning at nine."

Any attorney worth his salt wouldn't allow his client to say anything incriminating. Good thing Miguel was going to question Phillips. He was one of the best at reading people and had the strongest interrogation tactics on the team. Even with a lawyer, Miguel would be able tell if Phillips had anything to hide.

"Don't bother calling Albrecht," Madeline said. "Too easy for him to take the precaution of lawyering up, too. I'd prefer to surprise him, catch him off guard. Make him feel as though he's doing a great service by answering a few questions."

"Sounds like a smart way to handle it," Miguel said. "In the meantime, I want them under surveillance ASAP. Reach out to the field office in Spokane. I want eyes on Phillips."

Nick nodded. "I'll take care of it."

"Have we considered the prospect of an angry ex-girlfriend behind this?" Dash asked.

Of course she had. "I asked Jackson if he had any romantic entanglements lately. He claims there hasn't been anyone. Not even a one-night stand."

Dash gave a low chuckle. "I guess his whole world revolves around his kid."

"And his job," Miguel pointed out.

The unsub had just taken away both in one day. A devastating blow.

"An unrequited crush could also be a possibility," Nick suggested.

That was a tougher angle to explore. Jackson might be oblivious. Men sometimes were.

Miguel smirked. "'Hell hath no fury like a woman scorned.'"

Madeline rolled her eyes. "Have I ever mentioned how much I despise that saying?"

"Yes," the guys said in unison.

Shaking her head, Madeline smiled, refusing to give any of them the satisfaction of seeing her annoyance.

"The unsub could contact Rhodes again at any time," Miguel said. "We'll be monitoring his communications, but I think one of us should be on hand, spend the night at his house just in case. Since he went rogue once, he's capable of doing it again."

Miguel didn't ask for volunteers because he

didn't have to. Someone on the team was always able, willing and ready. This was her case. Her responsibility.

"It makes sense for me to do it," she said. "I'll eat, sleep and breathe nothing but this case until we bring Emma home." Though she doubted she would do much eating or sleeping.

"I'll have Caitlyn tell him to expect you and smooth things over if he has a problem with the Bureau maintaining a presence in his home."

Raised voices from the hall penetrated through the glass door of the small conference room, drawing everyone's attention.

Madeline leaned to the side of her chair, giving her a partial view of the hall.

"I'm only asking for two minutes." Worry was plastered all over Lorelai's face as she chased after her fiancé down the hall.

Liam huffed a breath, stopped walking toward the conference room and faced her. "Two minutes turns into five and then ten. The next thing I know I've wasted twenty minutes on wedding nonsense."

"Nonsense?" Lorelai rocked back on her heels, clearly offended.

Trouble in paradise again. Ever since those two lovebirds got engaged, it had been one fight after another. Lorelai had shared with Madeline and Caitlyn every wedding detail and inevitable problem that came along with it. Maybe the arguments were due to jitters, stress from planning the event of the year.

Or maybe it was proof that romance and happily-ever-after only worked in fairy tales.

Liam hung his head. "I didn't mean it like that. I'm sorry. It's just that there are more important things for me to focus on right now. This case is—"

"There's always a case." Lorelai crossed her arms. "But our wedding is once in a lifetime."

"Tell that to my parents, each headed for a third divorce."

"You and I are not them. I just wanted to know if you got fitted for your tux. They need time to make any alterations. The wedding is in two months."

"I know when it is and no, I haven't had a chance to get fitted. I'll get around to it."

"This is important, too, you know. I want everything to be perfect, for it to be the most spectacular day of both our lives when you seem like you could care less."

"I don't care whether there are roses or tulips in the place settings, notched lapel or peaked lapel on my tux, the style of the invitation or the endless list of things you want me to weigh in on. That's the kind of stuff you could ask my mom about to include her more. Listen, I looked at a gazillion venues, tasted food until I was stuffed and sampled more cake than I've ever eaten in my life. Why can't that be good enough?"

"Good enough?" The hurt resonating in Lorelai's voice had Madeline tensing in her seat. "I didn't realize you were doing me such a huge favor by helping to plan *our* wedding. Do you have any idea how many decisions I've made without bothering you about any of them?"

"No. Thank God for that small mercy."

David snickered.

Madeline was about to shoot him a warning glare when Nick prodded him in the side with an elbow.

"Can I get back to work now?" Liam asked.

Lorelai spun on her heel and stalked down the hall.

Not a good sign. Lorelai was never at a loss for words when it came to Liam.

True love was probably rubbish people clung to for hope, but Madeline wished those two, who seemed like a perfect match, every happiness together.

Liam strode into the conference without making eye contact with anyone. Holding a folder under his arm, he closed the door behind him and took a seat on the other side of David. His cheeks were a bright red from emotion. A normally vibrant thirty-year-old, he looked completely sapped of energy. "The last text couldn't be traced. I think the unsub was bouncing the signal around between cell towers. But I dug deeper into Mr. Rhodes to see if there was anyone who might target him for any reason, and I found this." He opened the folder and passed the contents around. "A couple of years ago, the Red Right Hand set their sights on him."

"I've heard of them," Madeline said. "Domestic extremists who take their name from Milton's poem *Paradise Lost*. View themselves as the embodiment of divine wrath."

"A pleasant bunch, spreading joy and cheer wherever they go," Liam said. "They've protested against ETC business practices outside of their headquarters while holding up signs that called Mr. Rhodes 'the Butcher of the American Dream' and even threw acid on the hood of his parked car after he was named CEO, but no one was inside the vehicle, so no injuries."

Madeline scanned the sheets of information. That seemed to be the worst of it, but there was a list of harassing incidents a page long, from sneaking into a cocktail party at a hotel and throwing a drink in Jackson's face to posting flyers around his daughter's school of him depicted as the Grinch, complete with photoshopped green-tinted skin.

"Apparently getting children involved isn't off-limits," she said.

"They don't officially claim to have a leader,"

Liam said, "but in fact, they do, and I found out who it is. Samantha Dickson."

Madeline turned to the last page. She stared at a picture of Dickson standing on a hill, waving her fist in the air, holding a bullhorn and firing up a crowd. The woman's eyes were filled with pure rage.

Ethnicity: White
Age: 26
Education: Bachelor's Degree from the University of Southern California
Parents: Sylvie and Donald Dickson, owners of Dickson Chemical Company

"She's *that* Dickson?" Madeline asked. "Heiress to billions?"

"Yep." Liam nodded. "Not that I'm sure if Mommy and Daddy are still leaving her their fortune considering she turned whistleblower on them. She reported the petrochemical company for dumping toxic waste that polluted a town's water source. The town filed a nasty lawsuit and Dickson Chemical lost millions in a hefty settlement."

"Bingo," Dash said. "Rich kid turned radical with a pattern of escalating aggression toward Rhodes. Her group made their unhappiness over him being named CEO unmistakably clear when they threw acid on his car."

The question was why. What on earth could Jackson have done to draw their ire? More importantly, why hadn't he mentioned it to her?

Miguel put the information sheet down. "She does fit the profile and has a motive to want the Butcher of the American Dream to resign."

"We need to bring her in for questioning," Madeline said. "Now."

Liam closed the folder. "That's where we run into a bit of a problem. We have to find her first. There's no known address for her. No utility bills in her name."

"What about the rest of her merry little band?" Madeline asked.

Liam shrugged. "I haven't had time to look into them yet, but I will."

This case was going to need everyone to work flat out.

"The group is still active?" Nick asked, stealing the next question from her lips. "Targeting others and fighting the good fight?"

"Yeah." Liam nodded. "In the past ten days, they've protested a restaurant for not paying their undocumented workers a reasonable wage and a cosmetics company for testing on animals. At the latter, they fired red paintballs at the CEO as he left the building."

Even if her entire crew lived off the grid, which

was a highly doubtful *if*, there was a way to track them down or flush them out. "Then we can find the Red Right Hand," Madeline said, "and Samantha Dickson."

Chapter Five

Caitlyn Yang inwardly cringed as Miguel rattled off her marching orders over the phone.

"It's imperative we stay close and keep an eye on him. His emotions are running high and justifiably so. The kidnapper will make contact again. When that happens, we need to be there. Hopefully he won't have an issue with Madeline staying the night," Miguel said in her ear.

Wishful thinking.

Rhodes had had a problem with everything else thus far. From how long it took the tech team to set up to the endless round of questions he hammered her with, demanding answers about the case that either she didn't have or wasn't her place to provide.

His frustration was normal. His anger understandable.

His entire world was hanging in the balance.

He was a guarded man who valued his privacy and was used to being in charge. Sitting around doing nothing while surrounded by strangers was probably the hardest part for him.

Now she had to be the one to drop the bombshell that he wouldn't even have his home to himself tonight.

"I'll take care of it," Caitlyn said, standing in the foyer, where she'd excused herself to take the call.

"As always," Miguel said. "I know I can count on you. Madeline should be there within the hour. She needed to grab some things from home first."

What did Caitlyn have to complain about? Madeline was the one who would be stuck here, dealing with Rhodes all night. No break to decompress and hit the ground running fresh tomorrow.

Caitlyn's heart went out to her. Madeline avoided taking on the role of family support during kidnapping cases. Not that she wasn't capable. Staying laser focused on finding an abducted child alive—always the burning goal—took precedence over the impact to the parents. Her job exacted a heavy emotional toll. Required a cool detachment to see things objectively and stay in control. Mix in handling the relatives and friends of victims, an already tough task which often pushed Caitlyn to her limits, and anyone could get overwhelmed.

It was a lot to manage. A lot for someone to be.

At times, Caitlyn suspected there might be a

deeper reason, one more personal, that kept Madeline at a distance from the families. Perhaps she was haunted by ghosts from her past. Had lost someone close to her.

In the five years they had worked together at BAU, they'd become friends, though not close enough for Madeline to share her history or reveal what had motivated her to join the FBI.

Whatever tormented Madeline also drove her to find and rescue victims, even at the expense of having a personal life of her own. As though her job was her reason for living.

"Okay," Caitlyn said to Miguel. "I'll hang here until Madeline arrives." She disconnected the call.

Her specialty was smoothing over ruffled feathers, whether civilian, media or local law enforcement, and Rhodes was testing her skills today.

Taking on the role of family support was usually effortless for her. Comforting the victims' loved ones gave her a sense of professional satisfaction that no other aspect of her job provided. The trick was figuring out what kind of support a person needed.

Everyone was different. No one-size-fits-all technique worked.

Her initial approach with the doting father had been way off base. The more she offered to do for him, the more anxious and snappish he became.

She had to go against her natural instincts, dial down her efforts to console him while minimizing the sense of intrusion when the tech team had been in the house.

Once they had cleared out, it had been touch and go with Rhodes.

The one thing that she had found worked no matter age, gender or personality was distraction.

She stuffed her phone in her pocket and followed the music.

Sad and familiar, the melody being played from the piano rose and fell gently, reaching deeper inside her until her heart ached. She slipped into the living room, not wanting to disturb him as his fingers glided over the keys of the baby grand in the corner.

Dear God. She never would've guessed that he had such talent inside him.

The way he played was entrancing.

He struck the last chord. The melancholic melody hung in the air, resonating in her soul, and goose bumps broke out on her arms. She wanted to weep.

Staying seated, he rested his hand on the top of the piano.

This was as good a time as any. "That was Supervisory Special Agent Peters on the phone. He would like to have an agent stay the night." She geared up for the rest of her speech. "The volatility of the situation—"

"Which agent?" he asked, his voice flat and low, keeping his back to her.

"Madeline Striker."

"Madeline," he said with a strange emphasis. A statement, not a question. For a beat longer, he didn't move. Then he swiveled around on the bench and looked at her, his face impassive.

Was he going to complain? Fight this?

One of the most important parts of her job was to reduce the stress for the agents whenever and however she could in her dealings with the police, the press and public.

Caitlyn raced through a list of potential objections he might make and chose the best proactive counterargument. "Once the kidnapper makes contact again, we want to ensure you're not compelled to take action you might regret. Especially if the form of communication changes from text to a phone call. With Special Agent Striker present we can manage an appropriate response, as well as act on any new information quickly. She's on her way here now."

"It's fine."

Wait, what? "Really?"

"Yes. I'll do whatever is necessary to get Emma back."

Caitlyn wiped the shock from her face. "I'll stay until she arrives."

"To watch me and keep me under thumb." He

rose. "Can I get you a cup of coffee or tea while you wait?"

"Tea, please."

THE NIGHT HAD grown chilly. Fat splats of rain pounded the car, accompanied by a long growl of thunder. Madeline drove her Volvo to Madison Park, a far more affluent area than where she lived. Her Wedgwood neighborhood was safe, affordable, allowed her to get away from the busy city center while the commute to work was still quick via I-5. But it was a far cry from the chic enclave of legacy properties lying on the shore of Lake Washington that many business executives sought to live in.

Out of all the high-powered, wealthy CEOs in Seattle, and they were in abundance in this city, why had Jackson Rhodes been targeted?

Better still, why work out the grievance through his child?

Jackson was driven, smart, self-assured without being arrogant. Capable of rising to the top. Whoever did this must view his love for his daughter as his weakness.

Children made you vulnerable. Opened you to the possibility of unimaginable pain. The very reason she never wanted to bring a life into this world. She'd watched her parents suffer for years, bore witness to how their grief ate away at their family like a cancer.

For all the guts she had every day on the job, she was still too much of a coward to be a mother.

The GPS chimed, indicating she had reached her destination. She parked the car in front of the house and killed the engine. Lightning flashed through the sky.

Storm clouds made the evening an unusually dark one. Everything beyond the wet windshield seemed to be dissolving, as though the whole world might drain away through some cosmic hole. She tightened her grip on the steering wheel, not wanting any part of herself to get sucked into the void, set adrift in the darkness, alone. It had been so long since she had needed to hold on to anything, but this case was dredging up the agonizing memories of that life-changing day when her sister, Kimberly, had been kidnapped.

For so many years, one question plagued Madeline.

Why Kimberly and not her?

Guilt tightened around her like a noose.

She'd worked so hard to move past it, to convince herself that she was stronger than the loss, than the pain that had nearly crushed her family.

Burying her face in her hands, she gave in for a fleeting moment to the dread and pain churning inside her. The memories made her want to curl within herself. Disappear.

Pull yourself together. You don't do pity parties.

That innocent little girl needs you.

So many in her field entered this profession as a way to do good. For Madeline, it was a way to drive out the darkness.

Dropping her hands, she hauled in a steadying breath and realigned her focus to one thing. Finding Emma Rhodes. Nothing else mattered.

She had to come to an understanding with Jackson that working together was in his daughter's best interest. Then she had questions for him, and his answers had better be damn good.

The rain slowed. The last rumble of thunder sounded farther away. The storm was passing. One good thing at least.

She leaned over to the passenger seat, grabbing her umbrella and overnight bag. After leaving the office, she'd made a pit stop at her condo and packed a few changes of clothes and some essentials. She would be holed up with Jackson for as long as it took to find his daughter and prayed that wouldn't be more than a day or two.

Madeline hopped out into the drizzle, hoisting the open umbrella over her head.

The rain crackled against the pavement as if it were oil in a deep fryer. She looked up and down the quiet street, taking in the surroundings. Only a handful of cars were parked along the curb. She noted makes and models. The rest of the vehicles were in driveways or she assumed the garage by this late hour.

Shivering against the chill, she walked up the stone path to a charming cottage set on a large lot. According to the GPS, the house was only steps from the lake.

The nip in the air had her hurrying up the wooden stairs and under the covered porch. She closed her umbrella, giving it a good shake.

The glass panes of the front door provided a view of the lit foyer and short hall that led deeper into the house.

Before ringing the bell, she sucked in the rainy night air, seeking a little more emotional distance. Then another deep, cleansing breath.

Still, she hesitated.

Compartmentalization allowed her to operate at the top of her game. She'd learned techniques to detach and deal with the emotion later—while out on a run, unwinding in the bath, during her kickboxing class, any time or place she wasn't on the clock and didn't have to be a consummate professional. That was the only way to do her job.

Yet all of her tried and tested tactics were failing her.

Something, or rather so many things, about Jackson and this case made it hard not to feel when the last thing she could afford was any sort of attachment to a victim's father.

Professional investment was necessary. An emotional one would only cause distraction.

She rang the bell.

Less than a minute later, Jackson and Caitlyn rounded the corner into the foyer, engaged in easy conversation. No one appeared on offense or defense.

Jackson opened the door. "Madeline." He gave her a smile, broken and weak, fragile as a wounded bird.

There went that catch in her chest, which came each time she saw his sorrow.

"Come in." He stepped aside, beckoning her to enter.

"Thank you." The space was bathed in soft golden light. "I know it's an inconvenience to have someone in your home, but I'll do my best to make sure my presence doesn't feel like an intrusion. With any luck, you won't notice I'm here."

"That will be an impossible task." His gaze locked onto hers. "This is a small house, but it would be difficult not to notice you even if it were a sprawling estate."

Was that good or bad? Considering how they'd left things when they'd last spoken, she wasn't quite sure.

Jackson had changed clothes, ditching the suit. He wore jeans and a cobalt blue long-sleeved T-shirt that matched the color of his eyes. The clingy material hugged his broad shoulders and biceps, stretching across a muscled expanse that tapered to slim hips.

All the oxygen emptied from Madeline's lungs.

She swallowed, tightening her grip on her bag. Never had she reacted to a man in quite this manner.

It wasn't as if she could click it on or off. A part of her feared blocking the sensation of feeling so routinely that she might construct a wall too thick and tall to be able to get through one day.

"The surveillance on his landline and laptop are good to go," Caitlyn said. "The team will be able to monitor everything. I should head out." She walked to the door. "Try not to worry, Mr. Rhodes."

"It's Jackson." His tone toward her had warmed considerably.

Caitlyn flashed a gentle smile, but Madeline noted it was more reserved than usual.

The evening must have been tense. Jackson coming home for the first time without Emma, surrounded by strangers. For Caitlyn, she probably had to navigate an emotional minefield, but if anyone could handle it with finesse and compassion, it was her.

Madeline turned to Caitlyn before she slipped through the door. "You might want to give Lorelai a call. I think she'll need to vent."

Caitlyn gave her a knowing nod. They were used to being the proverbial shoulder for Lorelai to lean on since the engagement. Both of them adored Lorelai and were happy to listen whenever she needed.

With a curt wave, Caitlyn was gone.

He locked the door and put the chain on. "Let me show you to the guest room."

"That won't be necessary. I can catch a few winks on the sofa."

"I won't hear of it."

He headed down the short hall, leading her past a formal living room with a piano. The dining room sat across from the kitchen. Beyond that was the family room, lit from the glow from the fireplace. Large windows overlooked the dark front yard. Next, they passed what appeared to be his office. At about two thousand square feet, the one-story multimillion-dollar home was cozy, welcoming. Tastefully furnished in a neutral palette, it was the kind of place where you wanted to sit down, have a glass of wine and snuggle in.

Finally, he opened the door to a room with a queen-size bed ready for guests. "There's no en suite, but the bathroom is next door. Emma's bedroom is right across the hall." Sorrow drifted across his expression. The muscles in his throat worked as if he'd swallowed gravel. "Mine is at the end of the hall."

Staying in the corridor, Madeline dropped her overnight bag on the floor inside the room, setting her purse on top, and kept her cell handy.

He leaned against the doorjamb and their eyes met, his deep and unfathomable.

For one quiet moment, they stared at each other. She fought not to squirm in her skin or shift her gaze under the unexpected jolt of power that came with that stare.

Why couldn't he get less attractive the closer she got? Instead, he was one of those men you couldn't help but look at. An aesthetic face that was all male, a slash of cheekbones and sculpted mouth. Blue eyes with such intensity of color she could lose herself in them. Hair that was thick and full. He was almost ridiculously gorgeous with a devastating presence that filled a room.

Before she melted into a puddle at his feet, she asked, "Can we sit down somewhere and talk?"

They needed to hash things out. Right now.

Jackson gestured for Madeline to follow him.

Lecturing him, extolling her success rate, trying to use her position to get him to fall in line wouldn't work on him. Only one thing would get him to trust her and treat her like a teammate in this because he sure as heck wasn't going to sit on the sidelines.

She straightened, steeling herself for what she had to do.

Chapter Six

Walking down the hall, Jackson led the way back through the house, sensing what Madeline was about to bring up.

She wanted to talk about the way he'd handled the press conference. Read him the riot act. Lay down the law. Make sure he understood who was in charge and how things would go from here on out. It was evident in her bearing, the way her tone had changed.

If they needed to clear the air and reach an understanding, so be it.

First, he damn sure needed a drink. Anger and adrenaline had drained from him, leaving him cold with a bone-deep fear.

Minutes had blurred together until hours had crept by since he had resigned on television. Still, there was no proof of life. No new text.

Only silence while he was forced to wait in purgatory.

Had he made a mistake? Had he ruined his

one chance to find out whether his daughter was alive?

No, no, he mustn't think like that. Following his gut wasn't wrong.

He shuttered the doubt. Nothing was final. Not yet. He'd created a loophole rather than backing himself into a corner he couldn't escape.

The monster who'd taken his daughter wanted Jackson's resignation to be final. The only way that would happen was to have evidence Emma was all right.

Inside the family room, he made a beeline to the discreet bar at the far wall. "Do you drink Scotch or brandy?"

"Brandy, but not while I'm on duty."

He pulled the cork from a bottle and poured amber liquid into two snifters. Crossing the room, he handed her one. "Calvados. Lecompte. You can't remain on duty 24/7. I got the impression from Caitlyn that you're here to make sure I don't do anything stupid. One drink won't prevent you from doing that."

Madeline considered him. "One." She accepted the glass, smelled the brandy and took a sip. "I haven't tasted Calvados this good since my last vacation, in Paris."

"How long ago was that?"

Madeline sat on the sofa that faced the burning gas fireplace. "I'm ashamed to say, but it's been too long since I've taken any time off."

She was a workaholic, the same as him.

Emma was the only thing to drag him out of the office. With one parent gone, he did his best to shower her with the love and attention that two would give. Sometimes that meant spoiling her a bit. At other times, he worried that he pushed her too hard to excel.

He turned from Madeline toward the fire. Closed his eyes, pictured Emma safe and warm and tucked into bed, waiting for him to read a story. Tears pressed against his eyelids. He recalled the sound of her giggle, the feel of her hair slipping through his fingers, the fruity scent of her shampoo mingled with her skin still damp from her bath.

Fathomless despair yawned inside him like an abyss.

Opening his eyes, the world blurred. He blinked back tears and took a healthy swallow of brandy, forcing himself to stop before he drained the snifter.

The doorbell rang.

Madeline shifted on the sofa, glancing toward the hall. "Are you expecting anyone?"

"I'm not. I'll be right back." He set his glass down on the coffee table and went to the door.

From the foyer, he spotted Brittany.

Jackson opened the door and let her in.

She stepped into the foyer, carrying a large brown paper bag.

"What are you doing here?" he asked.

Brittany tucked her straight black hair behind her ear. "Today has been a whirlwind. I haven't had a chance to say how sorry I am about what happened to Emma." She clasped his arm with her free hand. "I wanted to stop by and see how you were holding up. Thought maybe you could use some company."

"That's very considerate of you, but unnecessary." No one needed to make a fuss over him. Everyone's concern and energy should be directed toward Emma.

"I can't imagine what you must be going through. Not knowing where she is, who has her. It must be torture." Brittany's gaze shifted behind him.

Jackson looked over his shoulder. Madeline stood on the periphery of the foyer.

"I'm sorry." Brittany dropped her hand and shuffled backward. "I didn't realize you weren't alone." Her gaze bounced between them, a flush blooming on her cheeks.

"This is Special Agent Madeline Striker," he said.

"Oh, you're one of the FBI agents investigating the case," Brittany said. "There were so many police officers and agents at ETC earlier. I didn't think you guys would still be here this late."

Madeline strolled deeper into the foyer. "I'm

staying the night. The Bureau wants to ensure we have an around-the-clock presence."

"Really? I would've expected a police officer parked out front for that sort of thing," Brittany said. "Not an agent in the house overnight."

"Are you well versed in law enforcement protocol?" Madeline asked.

"I just assumed, you know," Brittany said. "From movies, TV shows, that sort of thing." She glanced down at the bag in her hand. "Takeout from Spinasse. I figured you wouldn't think about eating until you were famished."

How astute of her. He hadn't eaten since the Family Day event, but he wasn't hungry. The thought of food turned his stomach.

Brittany handed him the bag. "A few of your favorite dishes. You need to keep up your strength. For Emma's sake."

Jackson smiled at her. She was the world's best assistant. Always looking out for him. "Thank you, but I wish you hadn't gone to the trouble."

Brittany shrugged, throwing a glance at Madeline. "No trouble at all. Besides, I also picked up a late dinner for me and Aaron. Saves me the hassle of cooking."

"Who's Aaron?" Madeline asked.

"My boyfriend."

Another step forward and Madeline's expression softened. "Is it serious?"

"I should hope so. We live together and I

think we're ready to take the next step." Brittany flashed an unfiltered smile, then her gaze darted to Jackson and the light in her eyes went out. "I saw your press conference on the news. Since you resigned, I didn't know if I should go into the office tomorrow. Did you want me to take care of anything for you?"

Jackson hadn't considered that far ahead. His mind snagged on the thought of getting proof of life, unable to go beyond the dark hypotheticals if one never came. He ran his hand over the cell phone in his pocket. "Stay home, for now. Enjoy your time off." She was only twenty-seven, worked fifty to sixty hours a week and needed to spend more time with her boyfriend. A break would do her good. "I'll contact the chairman and make sure they find you a new position."

"Are you really not going to come back to ETC?" Brittany asked.

So long as he got his daughter back, it didn't matter to him which company he worked for. Emma was the most important thing in the world. "That's not up to me."

"This is so unfair." Tears sprang to Brittany's green eyes. "I'll keep you and Emma in my thoughts and prayers. If there's anything you need, anything at all, day or night, call me."

He nodded, though he wouldn't call. But her dedication was appreciated. "I'll make sure the chairman gives you paid leave until you're reassigned."

"That's so generous of you. Thinking about me at a time like this when you're being put through the wringer." Brittany whisked away tears with the back of her hand. "Try to get some rest. You need to take care of yourself." She opened the door and stepped out into the night.

Jackson locked the door and switched off the light in the foyer. "Are you hungry?" He held up the bag.

"I'm good. But your assistant is right. If you haven't had dinner, you should eat something to keep up your strength."

"I can't right now." Not when he didn't know if Emma was safe. Had she been fed dinner, or was her little stomach rumbling with hunger pangs? He suppressed the anger and sheer worry rising inside him like a tsunami. "I'll put it away."

Jackson set the entire bag on the top shelf of his fridge and returned to the family room.

Picking up his glass, he sat near Madeline on the sofa. She pressed against the side of the couch as if he'd invaded her space. They were an arm's length apart.

"If I've made you uncomfortable, I can sit somewhere else." He motioned to one of the slipper chairs a few feet away.

"No," she said in a rush, shaking her head to

emphasize the word. "It's not that. It's just…nothing. We need to talk."

He downed the rest of the brandy, letting the heat slide down his throat to his belly. Got up and poured another. Sat back down, this time an inch or two closer to her.

For some reason, the proximity unsettled this unflappable woman. As he saw it, that took away her advantage and gave him a fighting chance at staying involved in his own child's case. It hadn't occurred to him how much information the FBI might withhold from him until Jackson had shot off one rapid-fire question after another to Caitlyn, asking about the bomb, the statements that had been taken, the list of top suspects, the next steps in the process—and she had told him virtually nothing.

"Let's talk," Jackson said.

Madeline cleared her throat. "There was a misunderstanding between us earlier. This job isn't a game to me. I'm sorry if I made you feel otherwise." She shifted toward him, wrapping both hands around her glass. "This is my life's purpose. It's the reason I'm here."

He got the impression she didn't mean *here* as in his house, but more of an existential reason for being.

"I would never gamble with human life, especially a child's," she continued. "Neither will anyone else I work with. Not while I'm in charge of a case. I may not be a parent, but I understand what you're going through."

He looked up at her. There was an openness in her eyes, a vulnerability that hadn't been there before. As if she had lowered a wall. Now he saw what she hid so well.

Something haunted her. She understood pain. Loss.

"When I was eight, my sister was kidnapped," she said in a soft voice. "Taken from a playground while we were together. She was two years younger than me."

Shock surged like an electric current through his limbs. "The same age as Emma."

Madeline nodded grimly. "My sister was never found, but that was a different time, much different circumstances. Technology has come a long way in facilitating investigations since then."

The hell she had gone through as such a young child, and to come out on the other side without acting the victim or martyr. He had no idea. Then again why would he?

She swallowed and then went on. "I'm sharing this with you so you know that what I've been through, what my parents had to endure…" A stricken expression fell across her face, but just as fast melted away, leaving warmth and determination.

Jackson inched closer to her. He didn't touch her, but the urge to reach out and take her hand hit him hard. When their gazes met this time, it was more powerful than any physical connection. Never before had he experienced an instant common bond with someone.

Even one borne from tragedy.

"It's the reason I've dedicated my life to this," she said. "To spare as many families as I can that unbearable grief."

The perseverance and true grit it must have taken to become an FBI agent, choosing to face the same gut-wrenching scenario on a regular basis, all to save others. It couldn't be easy.

Madeline Striker was steelier and stronger than he'd first assumed, being one of few women in a male-dominated profession. While he understood her motivation and admired her dedication, her self-sacrifice to do this simply blew him away.

"On each case," she said, "getting it right means everything to me. I am fully invested. The entire team is committed to bringing your daughter home safely."

The way she said it, the promise in her voice, the sincerity behind the words, rocked him to his core, spreading calm within him.

"Thank you for telling me." Knowing that she did understand what he was going through in a way most others wouldn't changed everything. He wasn't alone. "I'm sorry about your sister."

Unable to resist the impulse, Jackson squeezed

her shoulder, for a moment, but with tenderness as well as strength.

Madeline was fierce yet also a little wounded. Maybe a lot wounded.

Taking a deep breath, she nodded, allowing his sympathy without bristling, and he admired her more for it.

"I've often wondered why Kimberly was taken," she said. "Instead of me. Why I got to…" Her voice trailed off, but he filled in the blank.

Live. Love. Laugh.

For more than twenty years she'd battled survivor's guilt. He couldn't begin to comprehend what that must be like. He'd been without Emma for less than twenty-four hours and he was on the verge of losing himself. Right on the edge of the abyss.

Having Madeline there, with her calming energy, grounded him. Kept him from spiraling. Much in the same way playing the piano did. But no one could play forever.

"I owe you an apology for what I said to you earlier." Asking her in the heat of the moment if she was a parent, like some litmus test, had been unfair. The emotion that had flashed across her face he now recognized as hurt. He regretted saying it.

"There's nothing to apologize for. I can relate to what you're going through. It's the flip side of a coin, but it isn't exactly the same."

He lowered his hand, grateful that they could move forward.

"We have to work together as a team, Jackson. That means listening to my professional advice, and if your gut leads you in a different direction, talk to me before you act. Okay?"

He couldn't pull his eyes from hers. The depth of pain, of affinity staring back at him, wouldn't let him go.

"Fair enough," he said. "I can, I will do that. I hope that means you'll keep me in the loop." Being kept in the dark would drive him stir-crazy.

"Sharing information is critical. It'll ease your mind a little and help us find your daughter. But you have to stop withholding information."

He flinched at the accusation. "I haven't with-held anything." He'd never dare compromise the safe return of his daughter.

"Then why didn't you tell us about the Red Right Hand and how they've harassed you when I asked you about enemies?"

What did they have to do with this? "They've gone after half the CEOs in this city for one reason or another." Others had faced far worse treatment from them. "They're just a bunch of tree-hugging hippies." A royal pain for certain. Occasionally, a PR nightmare, but nothing more.

Madeline shook her head. "They are violent domestic extremists whose beliefs lead them to commit crimes. Thus far they haven't sought to kill or injure anyone, but they're guilty of vandalism, cyberattacks, property damage and arson. We're trying to locate their leader, Samantha Dickson."

"She's a real piece of work." Unfortunately, he was well acquainted with her tactics. If he never set eyes on her again, it'd be too soon. "At every protest, she's rather vocal. Along with a young guy, Kane Tidwell. He was the one who threw acid on my car."

Madeline sent a text with the name. "Their pattern of aggression toward you makes the group a suspect, though we're focused on Dickson. What motivated them to target you in the first place?"

Jackson gritted his teeth, hesitant to get into the ugly details. "Andrew Phillips and the smear campaign he launched against me."

"This smear campaign, what was it about?"

"It started small and then snowballed. Andrew spread rumors amongst the employees that I was a coldhearted cutthroat who only cares about the company bottom line after I had some of our operations moved overseas and had all charitable donations stopped."

Madeline raised the expected eyebrow at his admission, but it sounded worse than it was in reality.

"Andrew also made sure I received a lot of bad press for it. Not that I can prove it, but I know it was him. Ever since, I've been on the radar of the Red Right Hand."

"Sounds like you gave a lot of people legitimate reasons to view you in a negative light. Is there more to this story in which painting you as the Grinch was unwarranted?"

He liked a woman who didn't hold her tongue and who cut to the point. "The company was on the brink of bankruptcy. Either we found a way to remain solvent or we were going to go under. Andrew was the first to propose having machines replace workers for some of our operations, quite ironically. Over time, five years to a decade, that would've saved us money. But we couldn't wait that long to stop hemorrhaging. I recommended halting our charitable donations, only temporarily, and sucking up the PR hit. Instead of machines, I suggested we move a limited number of operations overseas. The impact was bigger and faster. I also cut one of Andrew's departments. Video games."

Madeline tilted her head to the side. "Was the video games department his pet project? Something he was passionate about? A reason for him to blow up the Duwamish site?"

"I started that department. It meant more to me than it ever did to him. During a reorganization, he vied for it and won. He lorded it over me, rubbing my face in it every chance he got."

"Did you eventually cut the department to get back at him?"

Petty vengeance wasn't his style. "Of course not. I sold off the games to other companies for a quick, heavy injection of funds. Everyone in that department walked away with a very generous severance package. Half of them ended up making millions in the deal. I made sure to take care of them. It was a major win-win for everyone." Even provided the funds to expand ETC's reach in the industry.

"That doesn't change the fact you moved key operations overseas, which resulted in the loss of jobs. I'm guessing quite a few, and that earned you the moniker the Butcher of the American Dream."

The epithet still burned his gut. But that's what the Red Right Hand did. They called you cruel names and protested. Though the acid splashed on his car had been disturbing, not to mention expensive, to fix.

"Also, you did stop the company from giving to charity."

"Everyone at ETC would've lost their jobs if not for those changes. I saved the company and hundreds more jobs. I'm no Grinch." Explaining to Emma why some people thought that he was hadn't been simple after those horrid posters depicting him as such had been put up around her school. For weeks, other kids had teased her.

That had been worse than the acid. "After the most recent incident with the Red Right Hand ruining my car, I issued a press statement announcing that not only were we able to resume our charitable donations by Christmas, but that we'd double the amount from previous years. I thought that would pacify them, as well as doing something good."

"Dickson is one of our top suspects. Along with Charles Albrecht and Andrew Phillips. Are we missing anyone who might have a grudge against you? Are you sure there's no jilted girlfriend? Maybe think back further than six months."

Jackson snorted. "That's outside the realm of possibility. There hasn't been anyone since my wife, Francesca."

"No one, in four years?" she asked skeptically.

Hearing the status of his love life phrased that way even sounded sad to him. "No one."

"You must've loved Emma's mother very much."

Devotion to the memory of his deceased wife had kept him single? A lovely notion. Too bad the reality wasn't so picture-book. He'd never been honest with anyone about his marriage. Carried the truth for years like a dirty secret.

He was tired of pretending.

"I did care for her a great deal." Much more at the end when she had been sick and suffering than at the beginning. "She was a prima ballerina. We met at a fundraiser for membership donors such as me. It was only meant to be a fling for both of us. A fun distraction. She got pregnant. So we got married. Quickly, we realized we were polar opposites. Not even friends. She was miserable throughout the pregnancy once she had to stop dancing. Resented me because I didn't have to give up anything, even temporarily, to bring our daughter into the world. Then she got sick." And cancer redefined how he loved. "I took a six-month sabbatical to take care of her. She was gone so fast, Emma doesn't remember her." He wasn't sure why he'd told Madeline quite so much. He only knew that once the words had started, there was no holding them back.

Unburdening *was* good for the soul. Lightened the load he had been carrying.

"You sacrificed for Francesca at the end." There was unwavering sympathy in her eyes. "You've continued to sacrifice for your daughter."

He'd been single a long time. So long, he'd grown numb to the loneliness. Earlier this evening, when his house had been teeming with people, while Emma was missing, it was like a scab had been ripped off, leaving him raw. Forcing him to face the emptiness that had metastasized over the years. Sitting here with Madeline, talking, made him feel less alone.

Tonight, he needed that more than he had realized.

"I suppose I haven't been with anyone because I've been focused on Emma and work. Not much time for anything else." Dating required energy and effort he didn't have to give when Emma was a toddler. Once she started elementary school, he had no clue how to juggle everything. "I don't think there are many women who would accept that I already have two top priorities. Who would be willing to settle for third place?"

"Someone who has her own priorities wouldn't see it as settling, but as compromise. Give and take. But I get it." She nursed the brandy, indulging in another tiny sip. "There aren't many men who can handle my grueling schedule with odd hours and not sleeping at home when the job demands."

Only an idiot wouldn't understand. She was intelligent, full of drive, beautiful. The kind of beautiful that struck you at first sight but deepened the longer you looked at her. And she was out there in the thick of it saving lives. Literally.

"All you need is one," he said. "The right one."

Their thighs brushed. Their gazes connected in the firelight of the room.

Hyperawareness tingled through him, calling him to draw closer, like recognizing like.

Under different circumstances, when everything he cared about wasn't slipping through his fingers faster than grains of sand in the wind, he would've acted on it.

He got up and strode to the other side of the room near the window.

Leaning against the mantel, he drew comfort from the heat of the fire.

"At least we can rule out the possibility of a hostile ex," Madeline said, crossing her legs. "Tell me about your combative rivalry with Albrecht."

"Our relationship has always been contentious, but purely about business. We've gone in similar directions with the manufacture of products once or twice. Right now, he's vying for a military contract."

"The same as you. Could it also be for stealth technology?"

He shrugged. "I don't know, but if that is his latest breakthrough that would give him a reason to target the Duwamish site. Having me step down as CEO might just be for good measure, a smoke screen for going after a rival product that could win a government bid over his."

"That's what I was thinking. I wish there was a way to verify what he's working on. Confirmation of stealth technology would be enough for us to get a warrant to search every piece of property he owns and dig into his financials to see if he's made any large payments. Perhaps hired someone to kidnap Emma."

Thanks to Chuck's need to be in the limelight, there was a way. "He's having a black-tie cocktail party tomorrow at AlbrechTech to make a big announcement. The cocky bastard even had the gall to send me an invitation. He's the biggest narcissist."

"Literally? As in inflated sense of his own importance, a deep need for excessive attention and admiration, and a lack of empathy for others?"

"That about sums him up. His dad started AlbrechTech in his garage thirty years ago, building it into the *Fortune* 500 that it is today. Last quarter, Chuck talked the board into replacing his own father with himself. He's a cold-blooded snake."

Madeline frowned.

Whatever she was thinking, he wasn't going to like hearing it, but he had to know. "Please say it."

"People with narcissistic personality disorder are more likely to become child abductors. But that's usually in cases where the kidnapper is the parent. I'm sure whatever the announcement is will make the news the morning after the event. We'll have to wait and see."

To hell with that. This was a golden opportunity to get inside AlbrechTech, check things out and see firsthand for himself. "I'm not waiting. I can't." He raised a palm. "Please don't ask me to."

"You never hear the word *no*, do you?"

"It's been spoken in my vicinity on occasion, but somehow never directed toward me." He was persuasive and shrewd, had to be in his business, and he wasn't going to apologize for it.

Scooting to the edge of the sofa, she leaned forward. "We should expect the press to be there. The optics of you at a party wouldn't be good. You'd receive unwanted attention that could complicate matters for the case. For you personally."

"I wouldn't be there to have fun. Only to find out what Chuck is up to."

"They wouldn't know that. Freedom of the press could easily flip to freedom to be merciless. They'd have a field day telling the story of the father with a missing child who was kicking up his heels at a party. Misinformation, of course, but it'd sell a lot of newspapers."

He didn't care about getting roasted by the press, but assuming Chuck wasn't the kidnapper and pictures of him attending a party surfaced, then whoever had Emma might think he wasn't taking this seriously and seek to punish him further.

A hiccup he hadn't thought of, but for every problem there was a solution.

Madeline's gaze snapped up to something over his shoulder, her eyes widening as she jumped to her feet and rushed forward. "Oh, my God. What is that?"

Spinning a one-eighty, Jackson faced the window. He went slack-jawed at the sight in his yard.

Flaming lines that burned three feet long blazed on his front lawn.

In the darkness, four letters spelled out a single word in fire.

Chapter Seven

Madeline stood at Jackson's side and stared out the window. She opened her mouth to ask what the fiery word meant, but a flash of movement registered in the shadows off the left corner of the yard.

Someone dressed in all black, wearing a plain white mask with a hood pulled up over their head, turned and took off like a shot.

The unsub. It had to be.

Madeline withdrew her service weapon from the holster on her hip and bolted for the front door.

Heavy footfalls pounded after her.

She flipped a switch beside the door, bringing on the porch light, and had the chain off and was out the door before Jackson caught up.

With her Glock at the ready, Madeline charged down the wooden steps. She cleared the front yard, gun swinging in a careful arc as she made her way to the sidewalk.

She scanned the north side of the street. The left. No one was visible. No pedestrians out walking their dog. Nothing suspicious.

Jackson ran to her. A baseball bat was clenched in his hands. "Where did he go?"

His house was situated in the middle of a long lane. The unsub wouldn't have had time to disappear around the corner on foot. Not even if they were an Olympic sprinter.

They were hiding. In a neighbor's yard. Or a car.

"Stay here," Madeline ordered Jackson.

She darted into the middle of the street illuminated by streetlamps and looked in both directions. She'd taken the time to scope out the block earlier. Knew which vehicles had been there.

Did anything stand out? Was something different?

There! A black van. Parked barely twenty yards away with the quiet engine running, headlights off.

She locked onto the white full-face mask behind the wheel. The unsub was watching.

The engine roared, tires squealing on the wet pavement, and the vehicle raced toward her.

Her arm moved on its own, raising the gun— pure instinct kicking in. She thumbed the safety off. Years of habit had her sighting down the barrel, her left hand coming over to steady the

Glock in her palm, finger sliding inside the trigger guard as the car bore down.

Aim. Squeeze. You'll hit the bastard.

Emma. The thought of the child made her freeze. If she killed this person, the BAU team might never be able to find Emma.

Madeline shifted her aim away from the driver's head. She could wound the unsub and end this. She locked eyes with the person behind the wheel and squeezed the trigger.

Once. Twice. Three times. The darkness lit up with the flash of bullets. Holes blasted into the windshield.

The van swerved back and forth, still hurtling toward her.

Her breath shuddered in her chest, her pulse hammering in her ears. She braced for the inevitable pain if she missed one last time.

Steadying her aim, she squeezed the trigger.

But she was tackled from the side. Jackson had launched himself at her, hauling her out of the way.

A split second later, the van was breathing hot as it blew past.

The impact of Jackson's body knocked her off her feet. Tumbling with her, he held her tight to his chest. Momentum propelled them both down fast to the asphalt behind a parked sedan. He'd twisted, taking the brunt of the fall.

Madeline landed on top of him, the wind forced

from her lungs. Her shoulder scraped against something hard. Jackson's head slammed on the concrete curb. A groan tore from his lips. He rolled again, deftly placing her beneath him as if to shield her.

His considerable weight pressed her to the cold, wet ground. Instinctively, she had clung to him with one hand as they were falling, but she had managed to hold on to the gun with the other.

Her fingers dug into chiseled muscle. Their legs tangled. His face lifted, putting his lips inches from hers, his breath fanning her cheek.

For a heartbeat, everything blended into one. Fear. Adrenaline. The feel of the damp pavement. The warmth of his searing heat. His strong arms wrapped around her. The scent of his aftershave and burning rubber.

She got her bearings. Regained her breath.

Brakes screeched. The transmission ground, making an ugly noise.

Madeline slid to the side, out from under Jackson, shoving herself upright to peer around the sedan's bumper. Her vision speckled and then cleared.

The driver threw the van in Reverse, gunning the engine, and headed back for them.

She squeezed one shot off, hitting the rear door.

The vehicle kept coming.

Jackson grabbed her by the elbow, yanking

her to her feet. A wave of light-headedness swept through her.

They both stumbled up onto the sidewalk and back out of the way in the nick of time.

The van slammed alongside the sedan, metal scraping against metal, and then angled backward, mowing over the spot where they had just been.

She fired again. This time she aimed for the tires. Bullets pinged, striking steel.

The driver righted the car, threw it in Drive and punched the accelerator, burning rubber down the street. A hard left and the van careened around the corner out of sight.

Madeline's heart beat wildly in her throat. Relief coursed through her, but it was fleeting.

Emma's kidnapper had gotten away.

Madeline put her hand to Jackson's chest, thankful they hadn't been crushed by the van. "Are you okay?"

Tension rolled off him in waves. He inhaled, his muscular chest expanding beneath her palm. "Fine."

But he wasn't fine. Blood trickled down his temple from a cut over his brow.

"You okay?" he asked.

Her shoulder ached and the skin where she'd scraped it burned. "I'll live."

Lights started popping on in the windows of

his neighbors. The cops would be there soon. Surely someone had called them by now.

They crossed the street, making their way back to the house. She moved stiffly at first. One pant leg was ripped and strands of her hair had slipped loose of her twist, falling around her face.

He picked up the baseball bat that he had dropped earlier, and she holstered her weapon.

In the yard, they walked up to the flames burning on his lawn. They drew close enough to feel the heat.

Sticks had been positioned to create four letters and then set on fire. "'Pony,'" she said, reading the flaming word. "What does it mean?"

"It's what Emma wished for on her last birthday. A pony. I got her horseback riding lessons instead. This is proof of life."

Madeline took out her phone. Thankfully, the screen hadn't been damaged when they hit the ground. She snapped several pictures of the letters before the fire died out and messaged the photos to the team along with a quick breakdown of what had happened.

"What about the video I asked for?" Jackson looked at her with haunted eyes. "Do you think he'll send it? Or is this it?" His gaze drifted back to the burning letters. "The only proof of life I'll get."

Honestly, she didn't know for certain. "Every

action Emma's kidnapper has taken has been calculated and planned with one consistent goal. Hurting you. Torturing you. Manipulating you." First, Emma was taken right in front of him. That one act alone was enough to riddle any parent with overwhelming guilt. Then his pet project was destroyed. He was pressured to resign ahead of the deadline. Now this. A violation of his home, stripping him of any small peace of mind. All of it designed to mess with his head. "Not sending you a video would leave you to wonder. The imagination is powerful. Can conjure up all sorts of ugly possibilities. But you demanded to see Emma before your resignation is made official and you haven't. I think you'll be made to wait a little while longer. Then the kidnapper will make contact again."

Whoever it was wanted to stretch this out, make Jackson suffer, and Madeline feared they weren't finished with him. Not by a mile.

"But he just tried to kill me," Jackson said.

"Actually, the van was coming for me and you merely got in the way." The kidnapper had taken things to the next level. Attempted murder. Apparently, they were willing to kill under the right circumstances. That made them far more dangerous. "For the record, don't ever do that again."

"What? Save your life?" The hint of a smile tugged at the edges of his mouth.

"Put yourself in harm's way. Not for me." Part of her job was to keep him safe. Even protect him from himself if necessary.

Jackson closed the gap between them, stepping so close she had to tilt her head back to maintain eye contact. His wide shoulders and broad chest were like a wall in front of her. The rich scent of his aftershave, cedar and musk, had her softening again.

"In case you haven't figured it out yet," he said with the gleam of challenge in his eyes, "I'm not good at following orders."

"Oh, I've noticed."

"By the way, you're welcome."

The phone in her hand vibrated. A call from Miguel. Stepping away from Jackson and that scent which teased her senseless, she answered. "Hope I didn't wake you with the update." Doubtful since it was only eleven. The BAU team was accustomed to operating on little sleep.

"Are you and Jackson all right?" Concern flooded Miguel's voice.

She'd forgotten to highlight that they were okay in the message. "Yeah. We both are." Thanks to Jackson getting her out of the way of the van. She did indeed owe him her life. "Only some scratches."

"I'm going to have Dash check traffic camera footage and try to locate the van." A hotshot hacker, if anyone could cut through the red tape, or circumvent it to find an answer fast, it was Dash. "Did you catch a license plate number?"

"No. Everything happened too fast. But it wasn't a passenger van. It was one of those smaller service vans." She closed her eyes, tried to recall additional details. "A Ford Transit, I think."

"Okay. That'll give him more to go on."

"What about a description of the perp?"

"I couldn't make out much. The person was standing far away in the shadows. The white mask is what caught my eye. I only saw them for a second. Average height. Medium build. Nothing distinctive. Sorry."

"We'll track the van. Put out an APB." The all-points bulletin would have local law enforcement on the lookout for the vehicle.

As soon as two squad cars with flashing lights pulled up, an elderly neighbor across the street, whose sedan had been damaged, came outside.

This was going to be fun. "I've got to go," she said, wishing Caitlyn were there to handle this. "The police are here." She turned, glancing at the fire again.

"Go. We'll let you know if we find anything."

No news would mean bad news. A dead end.

Another thought occurred to her. "Hang on. One more thing. The burning letters. There's something odd about the fire. It still hasn't gone out. The branches are lying on top of wet grass. Never should have lit to begin with."

"I'll have Forensics come out ASAP and take a look."

"I'M HAPPY TO pay for the damages to your sister's car," Jackson said to his neighbor, Lawrence Travers.

Owner of the Wilderness Emporium chain stores, Larry was a laid-back fellow in his prime at just under sixty who loved hunting, golf and his wife, not necessarily in that order.

Larry waved his hand, dismissing the suggestion. "Don't trouble yourself. Sounds like you have an unenviable amount on your plate already. Looks it too from the gash on your head." He tightened the belt of his robe covering his pajamas. "Insurance will take care of the car."

Once Madeline had explained the circumstances, Larry had graciously agreed that they could work out the specifics regarding the damage themselves. The police had made a report and left.

Standing on the sidewalk in front of Jackson's house, Larry shoved his hands in the pockets of his robe. "Is there anything I can do to help you out with this nasty business?" He nodded at Jackson's lawn.

The burning letters taunted Jackson. Made the hair on the back of his neck stand on end.

"Do you have a firearm in the house?" Larry asked. "I can outfit you with a piece perfect for home defense if you don't."

"A generous offer, but the idea of having a gun in the same house as Emma without a safe to store it properly doesn't sit well with me. Besides, Special Agent Striker has all the firepower I need." Jackson glanced at Madeline, and she gave him a supportive smile.

"That's the spirit," Larry said. "Emma's going to be back home before you know it. Although in the future, you never know when you might need a gun. I'll have a Rapid safe sent over along with a 9 mm and ammo. The safe uses Radio Frequency Identification for quick access. You'll get a RFID key. Best level of child-resistant security. Do you know how to shoot, or do I need to set you up with lessons at the Emporium's range?"

"I don't need lessons." A marine veteran, his father had made it a point to teach Jackson three things at an early age: how to shoot, fight, turn every obstacle into an opportunity to chart his own path. While his mother had taught him to play the piano, giving him balance he'd never taken for granted.

A silver sedan rolled down the street and parked in front of the house.

"That must be someone from Forensics," Madeline said. "They should be able to tell us how the perp got the fire started on wet grass and why it hasn't burned out yet."

"You don't need Forensics. I can tell you that." Larry rocked back on his slipper-covered heels and puffed out his chest. "Smelled it from across the street."

"Smelled what?" Madeline asked.

"Tree resin," Larry said as if the answer was obvious. "Pine, spruce or cedar would be my guess. Fire equals life in a wilderness survival scenario. Resin is your secret weapon to starting and keeping a fire going in wet conditions. Highly flammable stuff. One of the best natural accelerants since it contains volatile oils. Easy to get and use. Great for all sorts of things and it's a renewable source. Melt the resin, soak some rags or strips of bandanna, wrap it around thick branches and it'll extend the burn time for a while."

Thirty minutes later, Forensics had confirmed Larry's assessment.

The fire died out and the man from Forensics collected the remnants to compare with the accelerant used in the bomb at the Duwamish facility.

After Jackson and Madeline trudged inside, he locked up behind them.

He stared at the nine panes of glass in the upper half of his front door. A damn window.

It was so easy to break in through a window in the door. Not that it hadn't occurred to him when he had purchased the house seven years ago. At the time as a new resident of picturesque Madison Park, he had thought the glass-paned door was quaint. A reflection of the carefree, safe neighborhood. Like the large bay windows in the family room that had never been adorned with curtains.

There was no telling how long the kidnapper had been spying on him before lighting the fire.

The vulnerability of every aspect of his life now stood out with stark lucidity.

He stowed the solid-wood Louisville Slugger back in the hall closet, where he kept it for emergencies. Though this had been the first time he had ever been inclined to use it.

In the family room, Madeline shrugged off her jacket with a groan.

"Are you hurt?" He wasn't sure if the sound had been caused by pain or fatigue.

"I banged up my shoulder. Nothing serious." She brushed long strands of hair from her face and turned away from him, draping her jacket across a chair.

Blood stained the back of her white silk blouse. "You're bleeding."

She twisted her chin over her shoulder, trying to inspect the injury, but she'd need a mirror to see it. Her gaze flickered up, meeting his, then higher to his head. "So are you. Aren't we a pair?" Madeline smiled weakly, a brief upturning of her mouth, her posture relaxing, her face open.

The sight of her like this warmed him, banishing the heart-stopping image of that van hurtling toward her.

Not for a single second had she shown a hint of fear.

Right now, she still looked tough as iron, but also shockingly vulnerable. An appealing contradiction.

For all her beauty, brains, nerves of steel, not to mention her incredible magnetism, it was astonishing to think she didn't have someone special in her life.

Such a pity.

Madeline cleared her throat and looked away. "It's late. I'm going to get cleaned up." She grabbed her jacket and headed down the hall to the bathroom.

There were plenty of fresh towels in the washroom since it was the one Emma used, but no medical supplies. He went to the kitchen and retrieved the deluxe family first aid kit. Then he made an ice pack and took it to the hall bathroom.

Jackson knocked.

Madeline eased the door open. She had removed her silk blouse and was standing in slacks and a black sports bra—the kind that didn't look like underwear or flaunt a ridiculous amount of cleavage. The women at his gym paraded around in far less.

"Thought you could use some Neosporin and a bandage," he said.

"You have blood dripping down your face, and you're worried about me?" She opened the door wide. "Get in here and sit down."

Jackson stepped inside, passing behind her to the other side of the sink. With the two of them inside, the bathroom seemed to have gotten smaller, growing far too cramped. He cast a glance at the black semiautomatic in the holster on the vanity. It looked out of place beside Emma's Disney-themed toothbrush and her hand towel with a picture of a unicorn.

Madeline bent over, lifting the cuff of her torn pant leg. He shouldn't have been surprised at the sight of a second weapon strapped to her ankle. The special agent came across as a woman who was always prepared. She tugged at the Velcro fasteners. The gun was more compact than her Glock. The polished nickel gleamed when she set it on the counter.

He closed the lid to the toilet and sat. Holding the medical supplies, he was now eye level with her chest. His gaze slid over the swell of her breasts, her sculpted arms, taut abs and wicked curves that showed the discipline of someone who rarely missed a workout.

Clenching his hands, he curbed the urge to

touch her, but he was so physically aware of her that it was like walking barefoot in the grass under a power line that sent a tingling rush under your skin.

He didn't mean to let his mind go there, but there wasn't a damn thing he could do to stop it.

"A good host takes care of his guest first," he said, breaking the silence and meeting her gaze.

Her eyes softened, and something sparked between them. Something warm. Something deep. Something strong.

"I'm not a guest." She sorted through the bag, taking the antiseptic and gauze. "I'm working."

Jackson fought for air as she stepped closer, leaning in until her breath brushed his face. He studied her features, trying to figure out what about them he found so captivating. Was it her high cheekbones, the flawless golden brown complexion, her well-defined lips or those riveting eyes, which seemed to see straight into his soul? Maybe everything—the whole was definitely greater than the sum of its parts.

He had never been attracted to weak women, no matter how pretty or charming.

There was nothing weak about Madeline. She was a force to be reckoned with.

She dabbed at the bloody gash on his forehead with a cotton swab, patting the skin gently. The tantalizing fragrance of her, vanilla and roses, stole into his lungs with each breath. He always loved the way women smelled, but her scent was so enticing that every muscle in his body tightened.

He closed his eyes, trying to shut out the sensations he knew he shouldn't have, but the absence of sight made it more difficult for him to think of anything else.

"You won't need stitches," she said, and he opened his eyes. She tore into a packet of butterfly bandages, closed the cut by holding its edges together and applied them. "You should put ice on it. Keep the swelling down." Turning, she chucked the gauze away in the trash.

The abrasion on her back was red and raw. Road rash from the pavement.

"Let me clean the scratch on your shoulder for you. It looks pretty bad."

"I can handle it."

Sure, if she was a contortionist.

"You're not used to accepting help from others, are you?" he asked. When she didn't respond, he said, "Quid pro quo. Only fair."

She studied him, her face a blank mask. Tension stretched between them, making the space in the bathroom feel even tighter before she nodded and faced the sink. "All right."

As he wiped at the blood, working toward the abrasion, she watched him in the mirror.

The second he touched the cotton swab to the

ragged flesh, her spine stiffened, and she sucked in a sharp breath.

"Sorry."

She grabbed onto the counter. "Don't worry about it," she whispered.

Brushing the antiseptic over the scraped area, he worked quickly. Her shoulders remained tense and a muscle flexed along her jaw.

He added a dab of Neosporin to the tender scrape, grabbed a piece of gauze and ripped off several sections of medical tape.

"Almost done." Taping the gauze over the injury, his fingers grazed her warm skin. Silky soft.

In the mirror, her mesmerizing gaze found his and didn't waver. Electric awareness shot down his spine, lighting up nerve endings along the way. Time suspended, and the primal attraction between them was undeniable.

He let his fingers stretch until his palms glided over her skin above the shoulder blades. Her muscles relaxed, her body softening, leaning into him. Something he didn't want to acknowledge and was helpless to suppress coiled through him. A dangerous combination of darkness and desire.

"Jack—"

His phone chimed, and the sound had them jerking apart.

A new message!

He snatched the phone from his pocket, his pulse in overdrive.

Madeline spun around and looked at the screen alongside him.

No video. I'm in charge. Not you. Not the FBI. This is all you get. Make your resignation official.

With another chime came a grainy picture of Emma. She was in a room, sitting on a bed with a gray wool blanket. Newspaper covered the wall behind her. Emma's brown eyes were wide with fear. Tears stained her cheeks.

"She's alive," he muttered. *Thank God.* Then a horrible thought struck him like a bolt of lightning through his chest. "Do you think he hurt her? She's been crying."

"Tears are natural. She misses you, home, everything familiar." Madeline put a hand on his forearm, and the sudden tightness in his chest eased. "She's scared, not hurt."

He wanted to believe that. Needed to. "Are you sure?"

"Yes."

He needed to contact the ETC PR team and have them draft a statement. "Once I make my resignation official, you don't think he would…" The words stuck in his throat. He couldn't bring himself to say the worst thing imaginable.

"Emma's going to be okay. Look on the floor. There's a Happy Meal container. On the bed—a doll, coloring book, crayons. She's in fresh clothes."

A pink sweat suit.

Why hadn't he noticed any of those things until Madeline had pointed them out?

"If her kidnapper wanted to hurt her, they wouldn't go to the trouble of feeding her, giving her things to play with. Changing her clothes." She tightened her fingers on his arm and squeezed a little. "Emma's going to be okay," she said again, as if the statement needed reinforcing, and perhaps it did.

Madeline took out her phone, made a call and put it on speaker.

The phone rang twice. "What's happened?" Miguel said.

Madeline relayed the message and details about the picture.

"We'll have a copy of everything at the office from the tap," Miguel said. "I can get Liam on it. Just to let you know, Dash hacked into the CCTV. There are no traffic cameras in Madison Park or the surrounding area, but the police found the van abandoned under an overpass near I-5. It had been torched."

Would they be able to lift fingerprints off a burnt vehicle?

"Damn it. Another dead end." She pressed a

palm to her forehead. "The picture needs to be analyzed. I want to know everything. Which newspaper is on the walls, clothing brand, any shadows, reflections, absolutely everything," she said with a desperation that echoed Jackson's own.

"You're not saying anything that I don't already know," Miguel said. "We'll analyze every single inch of it. No stone left unturned."

Madeline nodded. "We have to find a solid lead. And soon."

Chapter Eight

The elevator doors whispered open on the top floor of ETC headquarters. The hallway was carpeted in pale beige. The walls were light green. Miguel Peters stepped off promptly at nine and proceeded to the vice president's office. The outer wall and its door were glass.

Natascha Campbell rose before he'd gotten through the door.

The rest of the room was paneled in wood. The door to Phillips's office was wooden, blocking the interior from sight. As though ugly secrets were hidden inside.

"Good morning." Natascha walked out from behind her desk with a smug smile.

Miguel took in the young woman. Once again, she wore a gray suit: the jacket and pencil skirt fit snug across her slender figure. But this time, her auburn hair was pulled back into a sleek ponytail that sharpened her features, making her look even younger today. Perhaps twenty-six.

She was centerfold pretty, something he hadn't noticed in the previous day's chaos.

Natascha picked up the phone and pressed a button. "Agent Peters is here."

Miguel strained to hear the response but couldn't pick up so much as a murmur. The office door and walls were thick.

Interesting.

On the center of her desk was a copy of the press release ETC had issued earlier, regarding Jackson's resignation.

Natascha hung up the phone. "He's ready for you." Smile widening, she led him across the room and opened the door.

Miguel stepped into an enormous room that was lavishly equipped with furniture. His gaze swept across the table near the window, potted plants, a sofa, Andrew Phillips and his lawyers.

Plural.

¡Mierda!

One lawyer would be a pain. A team of lawyers would be a problem.

"Can I get you a coffee, Agent Peters?" Natascha asked.

Before Miguel could open his mouth to respond, Phillips said, "He won't be staying long enough for coffee."

We'll see about that.

Natascha left, shutting the door behind her.

Miguel sat in the chair facing the desk, beside

a gentleman in an expensive suit. The man was gray haired and thin and colorless as though the years had leached the life from him.

"George Grohs." The older man extended his hand but not to shake. A business card was proffered in between his fingers. "Mr. Phillips's attorney."

Miguel took the card. Across the middle The Grohs Law Group was printed. "You're not ETC corporate counsel?"

"No, we're Mr. Phillips's personal attorneys."

Big companies such as ETC often had a legal team deeply involved in various aspects of operations from exploring groundbreaking new products, supporting growth, to managing legal risks. Providing counsel for a vice president wasn't unusual.

But Phillips's going outside company channels to bring in his own team was highly suspect.

The other two, a man in a navy suit and a woman in red, who Grohs neglected to introduce, stood flanking Phillips on either side of him behind the desk.

This was more than a precautionary measure. Phillips was scared for some reason. Enough to hire outside representation that had cost him a pretty penny.

Dressed in a pin-striped tailored suit, tanned to an unhealthy degree, dark hair slicked back with too much mousse, Andrew Phillips shifted in his seat, not appearing nearly as confident as his assistant. A green smoothie in a clear plastic container sat untouched on his desk. The top half of the paper wrapper still covered the straw. "Agent Peters. None of us at ETC know what to think, what to say. We're all still reeling from what's happened."

Funny. He didn't appear distraught in the least.

"Mr. Phillips," Miguel said, sliding the business card into his pocket, "I'm going to record this interview and give you your rights."

The VP squirmed in his chair, smoothing a hand back over his hair.

Miguel set a recorder in plain view on the desk and recited the Miranda rights. Then he asked, "Where were you yesterday afternoon when Emma Rhodes went missing?"

The woman tapped Phillips's shoulder, a light press of her hand.

"I can't say exactly." Phillips looked down and away. "Because I don't know when she was taken."

"Let me clarify. Where were you between twelve thirty and one thirty yesterday afternoon?" Miguel asked.

Phillips shrugged. "Working. Somewhere in the building."

"Somewhere?" Miguel repeated. "You don't know where you were?"

"I'm a busy man. There was a lot going on yesterday. So many moving pieces."

Miguel took brief notes on his phone as well in case he needed to follow up on anything during the interview. "What were you working on?"

Another whisper in the VP's ear, this time from the blue suit.

"I was preparing for my trip to Spokane," Phillips said.

Taking a deep breath, Miguel tried to tamp down his growing frustration at Phillips getting coached by lawyers. What was he hiding? "Why weren't you downstairs at the Family Day event?"

"I was for several hours at the beginning, but I'm single and not all of us had the luxury of taking the entire day off."

"Many employees have characterized your relationship with Jackson Rhodes as contentious." Miguel studied him. "Would you say that's accurate?"

The prune-faced attorney sitting in the chair crossed his legs. "My client can't speak to the opinion of others. Move on."

Miguel cut his eyes from the shark of a lawyer back to the executive. "Do you like Jackson?"

"We're not friends, if that's what you mean," Phillips said.

"Are you enemies?"

The woman in red leaned in and spoke low in the VP's ear.

"We're on the same team with a common goal." Phillips flashed a shaky grin, his beady eyes gleaming. "The success of ETC."

"Did it make you angry to see someone fifteen years your junior promoted over you?"

Phillips made a small sound, a little breath of distress. "It didn't put a smile on my face."

"You're the only person with something to gain by Jackson resigning," Miguel said with straining patience.

"I didn't hear a question for my client," Grohs said.

Miguel gritted his teeth. "Do you find it suspicious that the kidnapper's one demand was for Jackson to step aside, effectively giving you the promotion you were passed over for?"

Both attorneys flanking Phillips leaned in at the same time, but he raised a palm silencing them. "I'm suspicious of lots of things. All-you-can-eat buffets, hotels with low ratings, that some prizefights are fixed. I can go on endlessly about my suspicions."

Irritation snapped through Miguel, but he didn't let it show on his face or in his voice. "Do you find it suspicious that you're the only one to benefit?" he asked again.

"Have the FBI considered that maybe the kidnapper's ulterior motive is to make my client look bad?" Grohs asked.

"No," Miguel said, deadpan, keeping the intensity of his focus lasered on Phillips. "We have not." With the lawyers buffering every response, this was futile. Miguel began to consider a different approach, a change in tactics. "Andrew, have you considered there's a six-year-old child missing? She's alone and scared and wants to go home."

The vice president's chair creaked under his weight as he shifted back. "Look, I feel bad for Jackson—honestly I do. I wouldn't wish what he's going through on my worst enemy. I assure you I had nothing to do with the disappearance of his daughter."

"That's enough," Grohs said. "My client has shown considerable courtesy in giving you this much of his time. I think this interview is over."

If this was courtesy, Miguel hated to see contempt.

Relief poured over Phillips's face, and he picked up his smoothie for the first time, removing the wrapper from the straw and taking a sip.

The more Miguel thought about it the less likely it seemed that Andrew Phillips cast the spotlight of suspicion on himself by kidnapping the kid and then taking Jackson's job.

But an irrefutable fact remained. Phillips was hiding something that required legal representation, and Miguel wanted to know what it was. "Actually, we're just getting started. And since I've been so courteous as to come to Mr. Phillips's office rather than giving him no choice but to answer questions in mine, I'll have that coffee now."

NICK JAMES ENTERED the observation room adjacent to the interview room and handed Jackson a steaming hot cup of coffee. The poor guy accepted it with a weary nod of thanks.

Jackson looked to be holding up well considering the holy hell he had been through over the past twenty-four hours. Though bags under his eyes, the five-o'clock shadow before noon on his jaw and the cut on his head showed the heavy strain he was under.

The press release from ETC announcing Jackson's official and permanent resignation had been released two hours earlier. But there had been silence from the kidnapper. Examination of the torched van had produced zero prints, and the culprit had been smart enough to remove the VIN number.

Nick stopped beside him and stared through the two-way viewing glass partition into the interview room.

"How long have you worked for Jackson?" Madeline asked the nanny.

Liane Strothe, a blond, curly-haired twenty-something, sat across the table with her hands folded in her lap. She wore funky catlike glasses and a long, flowered dress with Converse sneakers. "Almost two years."

"I spoke to the agency that placed you and they said you have excellent references."

Giving a shy smile, Liane pushed her glasses up her nose. "That's good."

"Have you been happy working for Jackson?"

"Oh, yeah. No complaints. The pay is great, the work is steady. It's so much better working for a family than at preschool. And I love Emma." Her eyes brightened as she perked up in her seat. The affection was genuine. "She's sweet and funny. Really smart for her age. Is she going to be okay? How is Jackson? I wanted to call him, but I also didn't want to intrude."

"Do you know of any reason why someone would take Emma to hurt Jackson?"

Liane's gaze roamed as she thought a moment. "No. I can't think of anything."

"How would you describe Jackson?"

The young woman's brows drew together. "I don't understand."

"Pretend I'm a girlfriend and you're describing your boss. Would you say he's hot?"

Jackson flinched as though the question had made him uncomfortable.

Liane gave a one-shouldered shrug. "I guess, if you're into that Norse-god kind of look. Thor isn't my type. I'm more of a Spider-Man gal."

Madeline had taken a shot in the dark and hadn't hit a target. Nick drew in a deep breath. "No issue of an unrequited crush with your nanny."

"Thank goodness for that," Jackson said, sounding relieved.

A lot of guys might enjoy it if their young, attractive nanny had stars in her eyes for them, but he clearly wasn't one of them.

"Where were you yesterday afternoon between twelve thirty and one thirty?" Madeline asked.

"At the movies. I went to see the new Marvel film at the Pacific Cinema since Jackson gave me the day off."

"Was there anyone with you who can confirm your whereabouts?"

Liane shook her head. "I was alone." She picked up her slim backpack that doubled as a purse, opened it and fished around inside for something. After a long sigh, she said, "I thought I still had my ticket stub, but I can't find it."

"When did you arrive at the theater and what time did the movie let out?"

Her mouth twitched. "I got there early. Maybe noon. I hate to miss the previews. It was done around three thirty, I think."

"That's a long time." Madeline's gaze slid over the woman, doubtful.

It sounded about right to Nick. The film Liane was talking about had a running time of 180 minutes. Three hours. Throw in previews and it added up. Still, it was easy enough to verify whether or not she had been there. "I'll be back in a minute."

Jackson nodded and sipped his coffee.

Nick left the observation room and headed down the hall. He rapped on the open door with a knuckle.

"Yep," Dash said, eyeing his state-of-the-art monitors with a frown.

"Hey, how long will it take you to hack into the Pacific Cinema and pull up security footage from yesterday?"

Dash's fingers flew over the keyboard. "Five minutes."

"I'm timing you." Nick waltzed in and strolled around behind Dash's chair to watch.

On one monitor the cybercrimes specialist brought up a black screen. Lines of code zipped across.

Between their tech guru, Liam, and Dash's stunning ability to crack computer systems and write code, the BAU almost always found what they needed if it was in the digital ether. Provided there was something to find.

"Was the new number that texted Jackson last night untraceable again?" Nick wondered as he watched his colleague work.

Dash blew out a heavy breath. "It was, unfortunately, but before you came in, I was doing a deep dive of the metadata to see if there was anything the kidnapper might have left behind." The camera feeds of the Pacific Cinema popped up, showing the ticket counter, concession stand and outside each numbered theater. "Child's play."

Impressive. "Less than three minutes."

"What are we looking for?"

"Not what, who. Liane Strothe. She claims she was there between noon and three thirty."

"Marvel movie?" Dash asked.

Nick nodded.

"Yeah, that's a long one."

"But a great one." Nick hunched over, getting a better look when time-stamped footage from yesterday appeared.

"You'll get no argument from me."

Nick zeroed in on the ticket counter. Liane Strothe sauntered into the lobby, wearing a purple long-sleeved top, jeans, Converse sneakers and had a backpack slung over her shoulder.

Dash typed something into the keyboard, and the screen shifted from the lobby to the concession stand, where she waited in line and bought a small popcorn and drink. Then they watched her enter theater number four. A few clicks on the keyboard, and Dash fast-forwarded. At three thirty, Liane left the theater, throwing her empty popcorn container and drink in the trash bin. "Her story checks out."

Nick thumbed a quick message to Madeline on his phone to let her know. "Thanks."

"No problem." Dash went back to plugging away.

Leaving the office, Nick stepped into the hall and bumped into Liam.

"Excuse me," Liam said with a grimace. Weariness added an edge to his expression and voice.

"Hey, there. You okay?"

"Yeah." Liam's frown deepened. "No. The wedding's off. I should feel relieved, thought I would, but I don't. This whole thing with Lorelai is messing with my head."

Oh, boy. "I'm sorry to hear that," Nick said sincerely. Before the engagement—correction— before the wedding planning, those two were so happy together. "Is this because of the fight you had in the hall yesterday?"

His cheeks reddened. "You all heard that?"

Reluctantly, Nick admitted, "We did."

Liam groaned. His mortification was obvious.

"Listen, we all understand couples go through stuff," Nick said. "I'm sure you and Lorelai will work things out."

"I don't know. I can't really think about that right now. I need to get back to analyzing the photo the kidnapper sent. I'm almost ready to give an update."

Nick patted Liam on the back, and they headed in separate directions.

At the observation room, Nick opened the door and slipped inside.

"Madeline is wrapping up with Liane." Jackson sipped his coffee.

Both women stood. Madeline was giving her the regular spiel about not leaving town in case they had more questions.

"We verified Liane's story," Nick said, closing the door. "She was at the movies."

Jackson's phone buzzed. Looking down at his pocket, he pulled it out and swiped the screen. Blood drained from his face and he swayed as though the world fell out from under him. "Oh, God. No." The paper cup dropped from his hand, splattering coffee on the floor.

Dread tightened in Nick's stomach. "What is it?"

"The kidnapper..." Jackson stared at his phone in horror, shaking his head. "He's not giving Emma back."

Nick took the phone from him and read the message.

You haven't paid nearly enough. I think I'll keep your daughter a little longer.

What the hell?

"I did what he wanted," Jackson said, tension

and panic sharpening his words. "Why? Why is he messing with me like this?"

Madeline and Liane moved into the hall.

A second later, Madeline came into the observation room. Her expression fell as her gaze traveled between them. "What happened?"

Nick handed her the phone.

She read the message, her eyes widening, her lips tightening to a grim line.

The unsub was determined to make Jackson suffer as payment for something he'd done wrong. But what?

Madeline clutched Jackson's shoulder. "This isn't unusual. The kidnapper has already demonstrated that they like to change the rules as they see fit. I should've expected this. Don't worry. This is a setback, nothing more."

The door flew open. Dash hurried inside. "I found something."

"What is it?" Madeline asked.

"A match on the cell phone that sent the picture last night. I couldn't trace the location, but I dug deep into the metadata. The same as I've done before. But this time the kidnapper got sloppy. I found a name. Natascha Campbell."

Jackson's face twisted in fury. "Andrew's assistant?"

"Miguel is at ETC now." Nick took out his phone. "He'll bring her in."

Chapter Nine

Madeline stood in the observation room next to Jackson. Behind them were Nick, Dash and David. From the updates rolling in, Liam was hard at work analyzing the photo. Madeline wanted him to stay on task until they either had a confession or Emma.

Miguel ushered Natascha Campbell into the interview room and sat her down in a chair.

It had taken less than twenty minutes for Miguel to read Natascha her Miranda rights and haul her in, but things felt a little off to Madeline. She preferred to watch this interrogation rather than conduct it. Sometimes distance provided clarity.

"I can't believe Natascha is behind this," Jackson said, shaking his head in shock.

Maybe she wasn't. She did fit the profile. Her boss had everything to gain. A promotion for him meant a promotion for her. Still, Madeline couldn't put her finger on what was throwing her.

"Am I under arrest?" Natascha asked. "Am I being charged with a crime?"

"Not at the moment. This is standard procedure. I need to ask you some questions about the kidnapping of Emma Rhodes and how you're connected."

"Connected?" Natascha reeled back in the chair. "I didn't kidnap Emma. Why would I take Jackson's daughter?"

"That's what we're going to find out," Miguel said.

"What makes you think that I'm connected?" Natascha demanded.

"You disappeared from the Family Day event yesterday around the same time Emma was taken. No one saw you for at least two hours. Where were you?"

"Working." She lowered her head and wrung her hands. "With Andrew."

"The two of you are hiding something. If you didn't help him take Emma, maybe kidnap her for him," Miguel said, and Natascha's jaw unhinged, "then what aren't you telling me?"

"Andrew said he'd send a lawyer. Maybe I should wait."

The lawyer had already arrived at the FBI office as representation for Natascha. A woman in a killer red suit. Caitlyn and Lorelai were running interference. Stalling. Miguel didn't need long. Maybe ten minutes to get to the truth.

"If you're innocent, you have no reason not to cooperate and answer a few simple questions. A little girl's life is on the line. Time is of the essence. I would think you'd want to help unless you're responsible somehow."

A classic technique. Most people who have nothing to hide felt compelled to talk. That it was their civic duty. All Miguel had to do was play on the emotion, apply pressure.

"I didn't do anything," Natascha said. "I swear."

Miguel nodded. "Then you need to explain something to me." He kept his eyes level, his tone cool. "Your name was found in the metadata of a text that was sent by the kidnapper. How is that possible if you didn't send the message?"

The metadata, the kidnapper making the convenient mistake of leaving it behind—that was what bothered Madeline about this whole thing.

"What?" Natascha's eyes grew so wide they looked as if they might bulge out of her head. "That's not possible."

"It is, if you were the one who kidnapped Emma and sent Jackson that text," Miguel said, pushing.

"No, no, no. I don't understand." Natascha's glassy eyes filled with tears. "Wait." Her brows drew together and her gaze roamed as if she had remembered something. "I lost my phone."

"Lost it?"

"Yes. But that was like two months ago."

A chill ran down Madeline's spine. If Natascha had lost the phone used by the kidnapper, two months was a long time for someone to plan.

"Where did you lose your phone?" Miguel asked.

"At the athletic club. Northgate."

"How can you be sure you lost it there?"

"I swim there three times a week. As soon as I got back into my car, I realized it was gone because I went to check my messages and couldn't find it. I reported it to the front desk, hoping someone might return it, but no one ever found my phone."

Miguel looked at the one-way mirror. "Get me verification."

"On it." David hustled out of the room.

"Why did Andrew have three lawyers during his interview?" Miguel asked.

Tears spilled from Natascha's eyes and rolled down her cheeks.

"He was afraid of saying the wrong thing," Miguel said. "Of incriminating himself. I bet you know of what."

"Please." Natascha lowered her head and wept. "It has nothing to do with Emma."

"Then you have nothing to worry about."

"Landing the position as CEO means so much to him. He doesn't want to risk losing it."

"What are the two of you hiding?" Miguel asked.

"Andrew and I snuck out of the Family Day event because…because we went back up to his office…to have sex." Her gaze slid up at Miguel. "You can't tell anyone at ETC. They have a very strict policy about fraternization. Especially between a supervisor and subordinate. If it's not reported to HR, it's a fireable offense. And the fact that we had sex in the office is considered gross misconduct."

"It's true," Jackson said.

"Sounds like grounds to have him booted from the position," Nick said.

Jackson rubbed the back of his neck. "I don't care who has the job. I just want my daughter back unharmed."

Natascha sniffled. "Andrew didn't want to go public with our relationship. So no one could know. He was worried that you'd find out during the interview and that he'd lose his chance to finally be CEO. It's all he's wanted since he started at ETC."

"A chance that he only got because someone kidnapped Jackson's daughter," Miguel said.

Natascha shook her head. "Andrew would never do that. I would never. I swear, we went back upstairs."

Dash moved to the door, stopping with his hand on the knob. "There are cameras in the elevators and halls. Only those on the first floor were on a loop. I have a copy of the security footage for the whole building from Rivka Molnar. I'll check it."

Madeline nodded.

As Dash hurried out of the room, Miguel continued to hammer away at Natascha.

"She's telling the truth," Madeline said low.

"If she's putting on an act, she deserves to win an Oscar," Nick agreed.

Madeline fought the urge to drum her fingers as her thoughts churned. "There's no way an unsub who's been so clever suddenly gets careless on this one thing."

"What are you saying?" Jackson looked at her. "Don't criminals make mistakes?"

"Sure, but this kidnapper has been meticulous." Flawless, thus far. "They wouldn't get this sloppy, leaving the metadata behind."

"The perp wanted us to find it," Nick said.

"But why?" Jackson asked.

More dots connected in her head. "Misdirection. They want us spinning our wheels and running in circles. If we're chasing after the wrong leads, then we're not chasing after them."

David and Dash returned at the same time, one following the other through the door.

"The athletic club has a record of Natascha reporting her cell phone missing," David said.

"What about the club's security footage?" Nick asked.

David shook his head. "Their security system only keeps the footage for thirty days and then it's automatically deleted."

Damn it. "What about the footage at ETC?" Madeline asked Dash.

"At noon, Andrew and Natascha got on the elevator, alone. He snuck a few squeezes of her bottom on the ride up to the top floor. The camera in the hall shows her kissing him, removing his tie, stroking his groin before they disappeared inside his office, where they stayed for a little over an hour."

Madeline bit the inside of her lip and turned toward the glass partition. They were right back where they started. Not a single step closer to finding Emma.

Her cell pinged along with most of the others. She glanced at her phone. Liam was ready to give an update.

She sent a message updating Miguel that they had verified Natascha's story and the young woman could be released.

The team and Jackson made their way down to the boardroom and took seats, but they waited on Miguel.

Liam looked awful. Hair disheveled. Unshaven. He paced back and forth as though he'd had too much coffee.

Madeline turned to Nick, who was sitting on her left. "Did Liam pull an all-nighter?"

"The wedding is off as of right now," he whispered. "I don't have details about the straw that broke the camel's proverbial back, but he's torn up over it."

Poor Lorelai and Liam. In spite of Madeline's reservations about relationships, she hoped those two would get their act together.

"Madeline," David said, "I don't know if you had a chance to see the update I submitted earlier since it's been such a hectic morning."

"No, I haven't seen it yet." All alerts she prioritized. The rest she would read as soon as she had a chance.

"I was going over the rest of the interviews, trying to find any discrepancies, and found one thing. Ten employees mentioned seeing four people as part of the catering staff."

"But there was only a crew of three," Dash said.

David nodded. "I know."

"Out of the employees, did anyone specify how many were men and how many were women?" she asked. They might be able to narrow down the gender. Reinforce her profile of the kidnapper or lead them in a different direction.

"There was no mention of gender," David said.

"Only that there were four people on the catering crew."

Madeline drummed her fingers on the arm of the chair. "That's how the kidnapper went unnoticed."

"Led Emma away right in front of me," Jackson said from his chair to the other side of her with his head down.

It was a key thread of information David had found. If they pulled on the loose end, there was no telling what else they might unravel. "Check with the catering company to see what type of vehicle they used for the event."

"Do you think it's the same kind as the one from last night?" Jackson asked.

The kidnapper using a service van to transport Emma made sense. Reduced the likelihood of anyone seeing her and wouldn't have raised suspicion on ETC premises. "It's possible."

David pushed out of his chair and was moving toward the door. "I'll go call them right now."

Jackson scrubbed a palm over his jaw. His brow was furrowed with worry.

"I know the last message feels devastating, but this isn't over," Madeline said to him, keeping her voice low so that only he could hear her. "They're not going to keep her. The kidnapper is toying with you." Wanted to drag this out and wear him down. Break his spirit a little more with each message.

"Because he wants to make me as miserable as possible?" Jackson whispered.

"Yes." And she was sorry for it, ached for what he was going through. For someone to use an innocent child as tool for revenge. This case was eating at her, digging at her from the inside out. They had to find Emma soon.

"Then I'm sure he's imagined what kind of person could hurt a child," Jackson ground out through clenched teeth. "What the psychological baggage would do to me. I'd never offload it, not for as long as I lived if something happened to her."

"You can't think like that." She patted his hand under the table, and he covered hers with the palm of his other, his fingers squeezing hers. "No one is going to hurt Emma."

"The kidnapper almost ran us down last night. That proves they're capable of anything."

"They have no reason to cross that line." Not yet. "We will find her." Madeline was willing to go to the ends of the earth to get his daughter back.

In his eyes, she saw that he believed her. She would do everything in her power to make good on her promise.

Miguel joined them, and Liam got started with his update by bringing the picture of Emma up on the screen.

"The photo the kidnapper sent was grainy, and it took some time to improve the resolution,"

Liam said. "The sweat suit Emma is wearing is from the private label brand for a big-box retailer that has stores everywhere. The store also carries the doll and coloring book. So nothing to go on there."

Jackson muttered a curse under his breath.

"After taking a closer look at the room that she's in," Liam continued, "I realized that there are no windows. I think the use of the newspaper on the walls was to hide that fact. Also, the floor is concrete."

"Like she's being kept in a garage?" Jackson asked.

"That's a strong possibility," Liam said.

Madeline stared at the picture. "Did you figure out which newspaper was used?"

"So far two. The *Emerald City Times* and the *Seattle Chronicle*."

"Are those recent newspapers?" Miguel asked.

"I couldn't make out the dates. So I started cross-referencing the ads and images that are visible. Found one dated last week. Here's an article that wasn't on the wall but was in the *Chronicle* for that day."

Jackson straightened as the article came up. The headline read:

New Emerald Tech Corp CEO Vows Cutting-edge Breakthrough This Year. Can He Deliver?

Whoever took Emma had a clear personal vendetta against Jackson, but one that was business related.

It took more than discipline and intelligence for Jackson to rise to CEO so young. It had required ambition. In her experience, ambition was a volatile fuel capable of great damage.

Maybe taking a closer look at AlbrechTech wasn't such a bad idea after all. Questioning Charles Albrecht was one thing. Getting proof of a motive was better.

Madeline glanced at Jackson. Stubborn resolve was stamped on his face.

David opened the door and popped his head in the room. "I spoke to the owner of the catering company. Their staff only uses one type of vehicle for events."

"Black Ford Transit?" Madeline asked.

"Yep, that's the one."

JACKSON SAT IN the passenger seat of the government SUV, more determined than ever to attend the event at AlbrechTech and see if Chuck was behind his daughter's kidnapping. Chuck had sold out his own father to get ahead. Would he sell his soul, too?

Madeline turned onto his block, headed back to his house. "I don't have anything to wear. After I drop you off, I'll swing by my condo in Wedgwood to change."

"Not necessary," Jackson said.

"It's black-tie. It is necessary. Unless you think this is appropriate." Madeline swept a hand over her shirt and slacks.

A change of clothing was essential and that was precisely what Jackson was relying on.

She pulled into his driveway. "Who is that?" Madeline asked, staring at the woman standing on the porch.

The slip of a girl had two stuffed garment bags draped over her arm.

"A stylist," Jackson said. "I didn't think you had an evening gown stashed in your overnight bag, and we don't have time for you to run home to get ready. I don't want to miss Chuck's big announcement."

"When did you call her?"

"I rang Petra while you were in Miguel's office talking to him about the party at AlbrechTech." He'd made *two* calls from the landline in Madeline's office since the FBI were monitoring his cell phone. "I've used her in the past for Francesca. She sent an assistant over with a couple of dresses for you to choose from."

Madeline arched a perfectly groomed eyebrow at him. "It's that simple. One call and the store comes to you."

"That simple. You're a six, right?" He opened the door and hopped out.

Madeline killed the engine and walked around the front of the car. "A what?"

"Dress size. A six." Being married had made him a good guesser in that department, but he'd asked Petra to send over options that ranged from a four to eight since cut varied by designers. All jewel-toned or pastel colors that would best flatter Madeline.

"I *am* a six," she said, sounding a bit shocked.

He knew it. "She also brought some undergarments to go along. I didn't know if a sports bra would work with the selections."

"Did you guess my bra size as well?"

He had. Guessed a 34C. Clearing his throat, he thought it wiser not to respond.

On the porch, he made a quick introduction.

"Petra told me to give you this." The assistant handed him a glossy black bag.

"Thank you." He took the bag as Madeline eyed him. "A disguise to throw off the press," he said to her and when she appeared satisfied with the response, he unlocked the door, letting them in.

Across the street, he spotted Larry leaving his house and making a beeline their way.

"Take your time, Madeline. I want you to be comfortable. If the selections don't work for you—"

"I'm sure it'll be fine," she said, staring at him.

Her striking face was a blank slate giving away nothing, her tone crisp and cool.

Once again, he had no clue what she was thinking.

Madeline headed down the hall and the assistant followed as the two disappeared around the corner.

Jackson went out onto the porch to greet his neighbor. "Hi, Larry."

"Glad I caught you." In the late daylight, his thinning blond hair and golfer's V-neck burn were pronounced. He sported khakis with a crease sharp enough to draw blood, a blue blazer with a yellow-and-green lining, a matching pocket hankie that protruded like a clown's water-squirting flower, and loafers with no socks. "This is for you, my friend." Larry handed him a ten-by-eight black metal case with keypad access, along with a RFID wristband and key fob and a box of ammo. "If I had to recommend one handgun for the home, it'd be the Glock 19. Great for the range, your nightstand and on your person for concealed carry. There's a Gen 5 inside." With a bright white grin, he tapped the top of the metal case. "I always store my ammo separately, but some folks like to keep theirs loaded."

"I appreciate it, Larry. What do I owe you for this?"

His neighbor waved a dismissive hand. "We never did get you a welcome gift when you moved in. Consider this it, a few years late." He shoved his hands in his pockets and rocked back on his heels. "I see the FBI agent is back. Do you keep the same one or do they rotate them?"

"If I'm lucky, there won't be any rotation." He hoped that was the case. Madeline had looked more annoyed than pleased. He might have overstepped by contacting the stylist, but that had been a risk he'd been willing to take. This was the only way to cover what he had done in making the second phone call, and he wouldn't make Madeline complicit.

"I'll say. I wouldn't mind having her around 24/7." Larry waggled his eyebrows, and his ruddy complexion deepened. "She's a looker, that one."

"Excellent at her job," Jackson said. "I couldn't ask for a smarter, more dedicated kidnapping expert committed to helping me get my daughter back."

The small grin on Larry's lips fell. "I'll leave you to it. If you need anything, let us know." With a wave, he hurried down the porch steps.

Jackson put the chain on, making a mental note to have his front door replaced with a steel one without a window.

Passing the guest room, he overheard Madeline talking to the assistant. From what he could make out, it sounded as though it was going well.

In his bedroom at the end of the hall, he closed

the door and set everything on his dresser. Pressing the RFID key fob to the reader, he opened the case, revealing the Glock. He picked up the cold matte black pistol. Lightweight with a low recoil, it was a solid choice for home defense. But he didn't have a need for the gun tonight.

Closing the case, he turned his attention to the glossy bag.

Madeline had made exceptional points about why he shouldn't attend the AlbrechTech event. All of them he had taken to heart. Inside the bag was a little something from Petra, the solution to the problem. A wig and fake mustache. Being noticed by the press wasn't on his agenda.

Also in the bag was an envelope—the contents of which were a product of his second phone call that he didn't want the FBI privy to. His contact had dropped the envelope off at Petra's studio as directed and collected a twenty-five-thousand-dollar fee in return.

No record of money changing hands between Jackson and the contact would exist. But Jackson would receive a hefty bill from Petra.

He checked the envelope. It contained exactly what he had expected. His plan wasn't above-board, nor was it definitive he'd have to go through with it. Always be prepared to seize an opportunity. That was what his father had taught him. A lesson that had served Jackson well for more than thirty years.

Jackson bathed and got dressed, putting on a tux. Applying the silicone-based adhesive to his face, he went slowly, working carefully to ensure the mustache wouldn't come loose at an inopportune moment later. He slipped on the brown wig that was streaked with gray and looked in the mirror. A different man stared back at him.

He drifted down the hall. The shower ran in the guest bathroom and the assistant was gone.

Jackson sat at the piano and ran his fingers across the keys like it was an old friend. In many ways, it was. A best friend that had never failed him.

He struck a few chords, waiting for the piece of music to choose him. Then he played.

Opening himself, he let his focus become so singular it was as if the music reached out and took possession of him. Let every emotion pour out over the keys. He thought of his mother, as always. But he also thought of Emma. Of her smile. Her laughter. Her tears. Of the little things that made her special. Of all the great things he hoped she'd one day achieve. She was his hopes and dreams wrapped up in pure, unconditional love.

When he finished, emptied of the pressure, he was breathing hard and fast. And this was why he played. So that he could breathe.

"Tristesse," Madeline said behind him, referring to the name of the piece, which meant *sadness* in French. "Also known as Chopin's Etude Number Three in E Major, Opus Ten."

It didn't surprise him that she knew it, but it did warm something in his chest.

"I've never heard it played so beautifully in person," she said. "Where did you learn?"

He lowered his head. "My mother. She went to Juilliard. Instead of realizing her full potential, she married my father and had me. She gifted me with her love of playing."

"And her talent."

Spinning around on the bench, he looked up at her and the breath stalled in his lungs.

A fuchsia sheath dress clung to her svelte figure. The vivid color contrasted beautifully with her radiant skin. A slit along the right side that ran from knee to midthigh was the one aspect of the sophisticated dress that wasn't subtle in its sex appeal. With her long dark hair flowing loose and wavy around her shoulders, there was only one word to describe Madeline.

Breathtaking.

"You look stunning." He stood and crossed the room. Her eyes were glassy with tears. "What's wrong?" he asked. "You don't like the dress or is my disguise that bad?"

"I love the dress, though I would've preferred

something black to help me blend in rather than stand out, and low heels would've been nice. Your disguise works. Quite effective." She dabbed at the corner of an eye. "You moved me. Your playing touched my soul. If I could play like that I'd never stop. Why don't you do this professionally?"

He frowned and the mustache tickled his face. "Could you picture me in a lounge playing for my supper?"

She squinted at him. "No, I guess I can't."

"My father hammered into me the practicality of pursuing business over music. But Emma is free to follow her passion, wherever that leads. She has been playing since she was three. She's quite good. You should hear her play." His chest ached with the desire to make that a reality.

Madeline moved to him and cupped his cheek. Almost as soon as she had, she dropped her hand and stepped back. "Should we go?"

"I arranged for a car. It should be here any minute."

"Why did you go to the trouble?"

"Force of habit for this sort of thing. Besides, my car isn't exactly subtle." His blue metallic Tesla was too recognizable to take to the event. "And I didn't want you to have to bother driving yours. You're going above and beyond already." He gestured for her to proceed. "After you."

Madeline smiled at him, warm and genuine, and headed for the door.

Jackson grabbed the invitation from the coffee table and slid a hand over his breast pocket, feeling the outline of the contents from the envelope. Under the best set of circumstances, he wouldn't have any need to use it. If push came to shove and he had to move forward, then and only then would he let Madeline in on the details. It wasn't the most ethical plan after all.

The last thing he wanted was to jeopardize her career and burn the personal bridge they'd been building. The possibility of it made him sick, tore him right down the middle. He'd try to avoid that outcome.

But he was willing to do absolutely anything to get Emma back. Anything.

Nothing was more important.

Chapter Ten

In the confines of the back seat of the luxury sedan, Madeline was highly aware of how delicious Jackson smelled. She breathed him in, telling herself to relax and focus on the job.

The car passed a throng of protesters gathered outside of AlbrechTech and pulled into a line to drop them off at the entrance of the building.

Madeline scanned the crowd, looking for one of their prime suspects.

"She's here," Jackson said. "Samantha Dickson. Kane Tidwell, too."

Someone set a wooden crate down and Dickson climbed up on top of it. She lifted a bullhorn to her mouth. "We will continue to target these CEOs and make them pay. We're going to turn up the pressure. Make them suffer. Hit them where it hurts the most until they've learned their lesson. They want to pretend like we're not here, as if they can't see us. Well, let's make sure they hear us." Her light brown hair was loose and free, flying wild around her face as she raised her right palm, which was painted red, then clenched it into a fist and chanted, "Hell, no, we won't go! Hell, no, we won't go!"

The mob circling her repeated the furious words.

This was perfect. Nothing better than a glamorous event with the press to lure the Red Right Hand like moths to a flame. Simply couldn't help themselves.

Madeline opened the clutch that matched her Tarik Ediz dress, shifted her FBI credentials to the side and grabbed her cell phone. She dialed Miguel. "Three guesses who is outside Albrech-Tech right now protesting."

"Samantha Dickson," he said, excitement ringing in his voice. "I'll pull the guys surveilling Charles Albrecht and have them follow Dickson. This way we'll know where she's staying."

"Make sure they keep eyes on her in case she changes locations."

"Of course," Miguel said. "I was just about to call you."

"Did Liam or Dash turn up anything new?"

"It's not about the Rhodes case. I got a lead on the terrorist suspect responsible for those two bombings last year."

Finally. Madeline knew precisely how much this meant to Miguel. The terrorist on their watch list had claimed over a hundred lives and evaded capture. Like every member of the BAU team, Miguel would risk his own life to find justice for the dead and try to prevent any more people from dying.

"I need to follow this lead before the trail grows cold," Miguel said.

She'd expect nothing less from him. "I understand. Be sure to keep us in the loop."

"Will do."

She disconnected and stowed her phone back in her purse. The chanting cut through the silence in the car.

"What reason do they have to be angry with Albrecht?" Madeline asked.

"Take your pick. From new facial recognition software that he sold to law enforcement, which they claim is racially biased, to drone technology for US Immigration and Customs Enforcement that's used to separate families."

"Drones," she said, and understanding of where she was going lit up in his eyes. "What brand does he produce?"

"Two. For the government it's ABC Daedalus, and commercially it's—"

"ABC Icarus." The *AB* stood for Albrecht. The *C* for Charles. With them being stretched to the limit on this case, they had missed a small yet important detail.

His blue eyes narrowed, taking on an iciness. "Were Chuck's drones at Duwamish?"

"The commercial brand, but that doesn't prove anything. They're very popular and widely available."

The driver pulled up to the entrance, stopping the car. Jackson got out, came around to her side and opened the door.

He extended his hand. She put her palm on his and he helped her out. The simple contact, a slip of skin on skin, sparked a tingle she couldn't ignore.

A flurry of cameras clicked, flashes bursting like fireworks in front of them.

Taken aback by the onslaught of paparazzi, she lowered her gaze.

"Sorry," Jackson said. "I should've warned you what to expect."

They hurried through the press gauntlet, neither of them smiling, both eager to avoid the cameras. There was a small white tent set up.

The moment they entered, an armed security guard greeted them. "Good evening."

Jackson presented his special VIP invitation.

When the man swept over the custom holographic foil print with a handheld scanner, a bar code that hadn't been visible before illuminated.

"What time is the big announcement?" Jackson asked.

"You're just in time," the guard said in an accent that sounded Russian. "Should be any minute since the entire board of directors have arrived."

Jackson nodded his thanks.

Another security guard took her handbag and searched it. Spotting her credentials, he flipped open her badge. He met her gaze, stuffed her identification back inside and gave her the clutch. A third guard, holding a metal detector wand, motioned for her to step forward.

If he did a thorough search, her BUG—backup gun—that was strapped to her thigh would set off the alarm.

Madeline extended her arms while the guard waved the wand across her upper body, moving lower.

As he came to her midsection, she dropped her purse. The guard bent to pick it up, a natural reflex he probably wasn't aware of. She lowered along with him, moving too fast and close on purpose, and their heads collided.

"Sorry about that," she said.

"No problem, ma'am." He also spoke with an accent. The guard grabbed the clutch, handed it to her and gestured for Jackson to assume the position.

A quick swipe over his body, and they were cleared.

"Are the guards always armed here at Albrech-Tech?" she asked.

"Since Chuck took over. He's paranoid to the nth degree." Putting his hand on her lower back, Jackson guided her into the building. The large, long lobby served as a reception hall. He pressed his mouth to her ear. "I'm fairly certain each invitation had a unique bar code. Chuck will soon know that I'm here. If he doesn't already."

That could present an unanticipated set of challenges or opportunities, depending on how the night went.

The decor inside was more lavish than she expected. The lighting was low and there were huge arrangements of flowers everywhere. Servers passed, carrying trays with flutes of champagne and hors d'oeuvres. Ambient music flowed and glitzy guests mingled.

"Now what?" she asked.

"We wait." Jackson took her hand and led her to the designated dance floor in front of a makeshift stage that had been erected.

The first strands of a waltz began. He whisked her into his arms, bringing her close.

Ignoring the tightening in her stomach that had nothing to do with the stress of the case and everything to do with their proximity, she looked up at him. She was a tall woman, at five-eight, but even with three-inch heels, Jackson towered over her by several inches. Despite the wig and mustache, his tailored tux did nothing to hide the bulk of his muscles. With his formidable stature he looked both debonair and dangerous. A tantalizing mix.

They moved easily, fluidly together. He was a

skilled dancer, confident in his lead. Was there anything this man didn't do well?

Relaxing in his hold, she struggled not to think about the feel of his wide, muscular body against hers. But it was impossible. He had a bold, dominant style that was inherently sexual. Not something he tried at. Simply the way he was.

There were hidden depths beneath that handsome face and chiseled body. It was almost unfair to the women of the world that he had brains, brawn, masculine beauty and talent.

He rubbed a hand up and down her back, making patterns against her skin. She wondered if it was deliberate or if he wasn't even aware of what he was doing.

His gaze traveled around the room. Not as though he was worried about bumping into Albrecht, but like he was casing the place.

"Is there something you're not telling me?" she asked, banishing her unprofessional distraction.

He lowered his head and his blue eyes connected with hers. His face was impassive, the picture of calm, yet he vibrated with energy. It was his hesitation that made her certain he was holding something back.

Madeline's stomach knotted and rolled. "Does our agreement about information sharing stand?"

His hand glided up her spine, his fingers playing over her vertebrae as he pressed his body to hers in all the right places. Lifting his hand to cup her cheek, he caressed her skin with his thumb, and her heart fluttered.

"It does," he said.

She wanted to believe him, truly. But she didn't.

The lights came up in the lobby, going from intimate to bright, and the music stopped.

"Ladies and gentlemen," a man said into a microphone, standing on the stage, "please gather around and join me as we welcome to the stage AlbrechTech CEO and firebrand, Chuck Albrecht."

Applause resounded and everyone assembled around the platform.

Albrecht jogged out onto the stage, clapping for himself, wearing jeans, sneakers and a blazer over a T-shirt at his own event. He was about the same age as Jackson, but lanky, average height, forgettable face. Someone who wouldn't stand out in a crowd. Unless he was wearing the exact opposite as everyone else. She could tell he was the kind of guy that people loved to hate.

He took the microphone. "Thank you, thank you. I know this is the moment you have all been waiting for with bated breath, for me to arrive." The crowd clapped and laughed. "Seriously, we're going to get to the reason you're all here in a second. But first, can I point out that we are about to have another rocking quarter?" Cheers and applause erupted. "Our earnings are through the roof! We are trouncing the competition like Emerald Tech Corp into the dust." The ovation grew louder. "No one can touch this." He pointed to himself, and the crowd egged him on with more laughter. "I would like to take a serious moment to acknowledge the horrific events a colleague is currently suffering. Jackson Rhodes, over at ETC, I'm sure you've heard. His daughter was kidnapped and one of his R&D facilities was bombed."

Murmurs rolled through the audience.

Jackson stiffened. His gaze was locked on Albrecht.

"I know, it's terrible," Albrecht said, shaking his head. "A tough set of circumstances. The guy was going to have a hard enough time already facing our next earnings report and his own limitations trying to cut the mustard as my competition. So, I've decided to offer a reward from my trust fund—not from the company—for any information that leads to the safe and speedy return of his daughter, in the amount of one million dollars."

A flurry of gasps turned into applause.

"What is he doing?" Madeline said to Jackson. This would only invite thousands of false tips to flood the hotline, pushing their resources, already stretched too thin, to the breaking point.

"Chuck is being Chuck. Showboating," Jackson said through gritted teeth. "I want to snap his scrawny neck."

"What can I say—I'm just that magnanimous." Albrecht put his hand over his heart and took a small bow. "And to Jackson, wherever you might be tonight," he said, letting his gaze travel slowly over the audience, "you're welcome, buddy!"

Madeline's lip curled in disgust. How could anyone be so pompous and callous at the same time?

Chuck Albrecht was many of the things she'd assumed Jackson might be before they had met— entitled, arrogant, a jerk. She couldn't have been more wrong about Jackson.

Compared to Chuck, they were night and day.

Once the crowd settled, Albrecht said, "Without further ado, let's get to the nitty-gritty of why you're here tonight. To celebrate. I have achieved something no one else has and every shareholder is going to make a lot of money because of it. Our fully self-driving cars have reached Level 5 autonomy with ten million miles and zero crashes." Thunderous applause erupted.

Madeline leaned in toward Jackson. "Aren't there already self-driving cars?"

"Not at Level 5 autonomy, where the car can drive day or night, no matter the type of road or weather conditions. Without any need for human intervention. This is major. An endgame for self-driving technology."

"Next week," Albrecht continued, "I'll have another announcement related to the DOD, but mum's the word until the ink is dry on the contract. In the meantime, raise your glasses to toast me and you." Everyone holding a glass lifted it. "Let's celebrate!"

Upbeat dance music pumped from the speakers and the crowd resumed enjoyment of the festivities.

"This is big," Madeline said, "but it's not in the same league as what you were working on."

"We don't know what else he has in development, but I need to find out. He has a military contract in the pipeline, and it isn't for his self-driving cars. There's more in R&D. Something that's close to completion. Or since he's talked about the contract as though it were a done deal, my guess is that it's already been finished and tested."

"I suppose we'll have to wait until he makes an announcement." She put a supportive hand on Jackson's forearm, knowing it wasn't what he wanted to hear.

"Like I told you at the house, I'm not waiting."

Before she had a chance to reply, Jackson turned and stalked away. Madeline hurried after him. Where was he going?

She stayed alert to their surroundings: the location of the security guards, who Albrecht was socializing with and the positions of the security cameras.

A guard at the end of the lobby tapped his ear

as though listening through his Bluetooth, and then circled around toward the crowd away from a door that led outside. Jackson homed in on the movement and headed for the exit that was far from the crowd.

A red roll 'n' pole sign warned of restricted access.

Ignoring the posted sign, he pushed through the door and she followed close behind him.

Fresh air hit them. The serenity and distance from the crowd was welcomed.

"What are we doing?" she asked.

Jackson pointed to a patch of trees at the rear of AlbrechTech headquarters. A lit path ran through the center of the woods, leading somewhere.

He started moving down the walkway adjacent to the building, headed in the direction of the unknown.

"What's out there?" she asked.

"On the other side of the thicket is the R&D facility." He kept walking. "The equivalent of my Duwamish site."

"How do you know?" she whispered. "Have you seen it?"

"Only aerial shots of the building, but inside information from a contact confirmed it. Whatever military-related project Chuck is working on is out there," he said, his voice low.

As they approached the corner of the building, the sound of footfalls drew near.

There must have been guards on patrol. One was headed their way.

Madeline grabbed Jackson by the lapels, yanking him to her as she rose on the balls of her feet and kissed him, long and slow. Without hesitation, he took her lead, wrapping his arms around her like they were a couple.

A guard came around the corner and shuffled to a stop. He cleared his throat quite forcibly. "No one is allowed out here."

Jackson pulled his lips from hers and lifted his head. "Give me a couple of minutes to take advantage of this opportunity, if you know what I'm saying."

The armed guard flattened his mouth. The bulge of the gun in his shoulder holster was obvious under his jacket. "The party is inside."

"And so is her husband," Jackson said. "I'm an important shareholder. All I need is five minutes and I'll be sure to let Chuck know how outstanding his security team is. Or I can make recommendations for changes. Your choice."

The armed guard looked around, his mouth twitching. "Two minutes. Not five. When I pass by again, you better not be here."

Jackson gave a suave smile. "I guarantee we won't." He brought his mouth down to her collarbone and nibbled up her neck to her ear, sending a frisson of desire skittering through her. "We better make it believable." The gravelly whisper was like a hot finger drawn down her spine.

He pulled her in a tight embrace as the guard began to walk away.

With one hand at the small of her back, he lowered his lips to hers. She welcomed the hot slide of his tongue against hers, wanting to taste him again as she drove her fingers into his hair. His mouth was warm and firm, more possessive than persuasive, making her pulse quicken and pound through her body down to her core.

The clunk of the guard's shoes disappeared around the corner.

But Jackson didn't stop, and neither did she.

The kiss grew rough and urgent. His hands clenched, pulling her ever closer.

She pressed against him, not knowing if this one chance might be her only and last. He pushed her back against the wall. The glass behind her was smooth and cold, causing her to shiver, but Jackson's clever hands molding to her ignited something inside her. She wanted more than a kiss. So much more.

Another minute of this and the guard would be the least of their problems.

"Jackson," she gasped, breaking the kiss. With the breath shuddering in her lungs, she looked up at him. His gaze was scorching. "The guard is gone."

Everything shifted in his eyes, turning sober and wary. Now full of something that sent a chill through her. Determination. "I have to go," he said.

"*We*, you mean."

"It's too risky for you to go with me. Head back inside. I'll check out what's in the R&D facility and come straight back."

Was this a joke? "You're not going anywhere without me."

"It's not safe for you. You shouldn't be involved in what I'm about to do next. Trust me." He cupped her chin and kissed her forehead. "We don't have time to argue. Please do as I say. Go inside."

Turning from her, Jackson ran to the corner of the building. He looked around and then he darted down a hill, avoiding the lit path, and disappeared into the darkness.

Unbelievable. Did he really think she'd be a *good girl* and do as she was told?

Madeline slipped off her shoes to keep her heels from making a racket against the paved path and chased after him. She passed a sign that read:

Stop. Authorized Personnel Only Beyond This Point. Trespassers Will Be Shot.

Once her bare feet hit the cool grass, she sprinted as fast as she could until she hit the tree line. Wood cracked and a warm line of blood scored her arm.

Stopping beside a tree, she put her shoes back on and searched the darkness.

Jackson was nowhere to be seen.

Damn it. Where was he? And how big was this property?

She guessed an acre, maybe two, at least.

A palm slid over her mouth, and she reflexively threw an elbow toward the person's gut.

Jackson snared her arm, blocking the blow as he came up behind her. He'd managed to get the drop on her. The man was stealthy, too. She would have to add that to the growing list of his annoying traits.

"I knew you'd follow me," he growled.

She swatted his hand from her face. "*You're* upset with *me*?" she whispered.

"You didn't listen." He moved downhill at a quick pace through the thicket, trekking parallel to the illuminated path.

Madeline hurried to catch up with him, doing her best to balance on the killer heels. "You simply took off with no explanation."

"I considered telling you my plan, per our information-sharing agreement. Then I realized it wasn't fair to put you in that position."

"You mean the position I'm in now? But in-

stead of having all the facts, I'm going in blind."
She tripped over a tree root and stumbled.

Jackson caught her by the elbow, saving her
from a nasty face-plant, and steadied her. "You
weren't supposed to be going in at all. I was
keeping you in the dark for your own good. I
decided the less you knew, the better in the long
run," he said. "That way you would have plausible deniability."

What damnable action was he planning to
commit? "Did you make that decision for my
own good before or after you kissed me?"

A smile curved Jackson's mouth, but Madeline
caught the tightening of suppressed anger in it as
he sliced a look at her. "Does it matter?"

To her, it did.

They cleared the woods and came out to a
glade. There was a building, not unlike the one
at Duwamish, sitting amid the tall trees.

"There'll be a sophisticated security system,"
she said. "We won't be able to simply waltz in
and look around."

"I'm aware and have prepared accordingly."
He took her hand, and they ran to the double
doors.

As he reached into his left breast pocket and
drew something out, she looked around for security cameras. Two were trained on the entrance,
where they stood. Red blinking lights on sev-

eral trees around the perimeter indicated there were more.

They wouldn't have long.

Jackson produced an entry card and swiped it through the reader.

"How did you come by that?" she asked.

The red light on the sensor flashed to green. The door unlocked with a click.

He opened the door and ushered her inside. "The less you know, the better." He slipped the keycard back into his jacket.

"Right. Plausible deniability," she said. "Which will mean nothing if we don't hurry up and get out of here before security guards show up."

A low whooshing noise captured her attention. A second later, the ten degree drop in temperature from outside registered. The sound was the cooling system recirculating the air.

They stepped forward, triggering motion sensors, and overhead lights popped on, bathing the space in bright white light.

"I'd say we have about two minutes before we have company," she said.

He nodded. "Come on."

They headed down the corridor. Labs lined either side of the hall that led to a large open bay. Beyond the glass walls of the workrooms, there were prototypes of new drones, biometric devices, semiconductors for a video gaming platform and equipment connected to a replica of a sink with water lines for what she guessed was the development of smart water tech.

"Do you see anything at all that could be stealth technology?" Madeline asked.

Getting closer to one of the rooms, he said, "No."

At the end of the corridor, they entered the large bay and stared at the centerpiece.

A military tank.

"How did I not guess?" Jackson said. "Chuck's contract with the DOD is for self-driving tanks." Slamming his eyes shut, he hung his head.

"Are you sure? Maybe it's stealth technology for tanks."

A look of defeat shrouded his face as he shook his head. "Chuck achieved Level 5 autonomy for self-driving vehicles. This is the next logical step. The most efficient one for the greatest profit in the least amount of time. Of course the military would jump at the chance to get their hands on this." Clenching his hands, he swore. "I had this all wrong."

Chuck didn't have a motive to torch Jackson's facility, and after the speech he'd given, Madeline didn't see the rival CEO as someone who would stoop to kidnapping to be top dog. The self-aggrandizing blowhard Chuck Albrecht didn't think he had to resort to such drastic measures because he already viewed himself as the best.

"He didn't kidnap Emma," Jackson said in a harsh whisper, voicing her thoughts.

"No, I don't think he did." Another dead end. She could only imagine how crushed he must be. The investigation process wasn't easy, but it worked. At least Albrecht had been eliminated as a suspect.

"Then who has my daughter?"

Madeline wished she had the answer. Looking around, she noted the cameras in the bay. "We have to leave. Now."

Their time was up. She took his arm and tugged him back to the corridor.

They hustled down the hallway.

At the door, Jackson used the keycard to unlock it. The night was quiet. The air still. But Madeline knew it wouldn't last.

They dashed to the woods, steering clear of the path. As they reached the tree line, shouts and noise suppressed gunfire erupted.

Madeline shoved Jackson behind a tree, taking cover with him.

They were too late. Security was onto them.

From the sound of it, at least three guards, using weapons with silencers, were in pursuit. The suppressors flattened the noise of the gunshots but didn't eliminate it entirely.

Madeline screamed, "Federal agent! Federal agent! Don't shoot!" She removed her badge from her purse in preparation to show her credentials.

"Stay here, out of the line of fire," she said to Jackson. "I don't want you getting shot by these trigger-happy Neanderthals."

With hands raised, she stepped out from behind the tree.

Three men snaked through the woods, headed straight for them and opened fire.

Bullets split the air and peppered into a nearby tree.

Madeline dived back behind the tree with Jackson. Her skull prickled. Had they not heard her? "FBI! Don't shoot!" she said at the top of her lungs.

More bullets smacked into a tree less than a foot above her.

Her knees weakened a little at the realization that the guards had heard her identify herself. But they didn't care. Because they didn't have to.

She was the one in the wrong. Trespassing on private property. Searching a building without a warrant. In the aftermath, they could spin the story however they wanted, and a good lawyer would get them off scot-free.

Bastards!

Madeline grabbed her BUG. The Beretta Nano was sleek, thin and compact, but only offered seven rounds. Each shot needed to count.

If that was the game they wanted to play…

She ducked low, peeking around the base of the tree. Took aim. Fired.

The single shot hit a guard through the right upper arm. His weapon dropped to the ground, and he grabbed hold of his perforated biceps as he shouted in agony.

...then she'd play.

Chapter Eleven

I should've brought the gun after all.

Adrenaline ramped up Jackson's heartbeat, had the tight muscle hammering in his chest. The new rush of raw energy catapulted him into fight-or-flight mode. That was the thing about fear: the right amount could help you. Made you think clearer, faster, got you ready to tackle anything that might come your way. But too much fear could cause you to make a mistake. At a time like now, that could be fatal.

"Don't move," Madeline ordered. Then she took off, darting to a new position.

Glancing around the tree to assess the situation, Jackson did his damnedest not to expose too much of his head and invite a bullet.

One of the guards noticed Madeline and aimed at her. She fired first, and the guard dropped to the grass, clutching his knee. Seconds later, she vanished behind a cluster of trees.

The unsuppressed report of her weapon was

shockingly loud compared to the shots discharged from the guns with silencers. It would capture the attention of everyone at the party.

Four additional guards were already rushing down the lit path. They cut into the woods, charging toward the action.

He and Madeline were outnumbered. Outgunned. Outmaneuvered. Still, Jackson had to do something to help her. Even if it meant taking a bullet to keep her from getting hurt. He'd created this mess and had to make sure she got out of it unscathed.

Calculating his chances, he seized an opening and worked his way from tree to tree. Bullets snapped and pinged. One whizzed so close to his head, he was forced to duck back behind a large oak. But he refused to stop moving until he caught sight of Madeline.

She had put down a third guard, once more without killing him.

Jackson was in genuine awe of her skill and restraint.

A burly guard, tall and thick, circled around behind Madeline, trying to sneak up on her. Perhaps to shoot her in the back. Like a coward.

The hulking man was six-five and a solid 250 pounds of pure muscle.

Jackson couldn't dodge a bullet. Nobody could. But one on one, in a tussle, Jackson could take him. Training, practice, size, all of it was a determining factor, but the key to a good fighter was natural ability. Quick reflexes and hand-eye coordination were two things Jackson had been born with. That didn't even take into account the years of training his father had given him.

The huge guard maneuvered past two more trees, drawing closer. He lifted his weapon, sights trained on Madeline.

Jackson bolted forward and slid feetfirst into the shooter, his heels connecting with knee joints that bent sidewise in an unnatural way. Bullets rocketed up to the sky, and the guy fell on top of him. Jackson flipped them both over, putting the bruiser's back to the ground. Without slowing for a second, Jackson slammed his forearm across the big man's face, breaking his nose.

Scrambling to his feet, Jackson kicked the man's weapon away.

Madeline had wounded a fourth man. Shot him in the shoulder. After disarming him, she grabbed him by the back of the collar and positioned him in front of herself, like a human shield. Her movements were quick and precise, but as smooth and practiced as a dance.

The remaining guards—Jackson counted three—closed in, focusing their aim on him.

"If you shoot him," Madeline said, gesturing to Jackson, "I'll make sure all of you are hospitalized." Her eyes remained flat and cool. "Not merely stopped with a flesh wound. But hospitalized. As in requiring serious pain meds and physical therapy for a very long time."

The guards exchanged glances and decided on taking defensive positions rather than pulling their triggers.

"Get your boss down here immediately," Madeline said, flashing her badge. "Tell him Special Agent Madeline Striker would like to have a chat about his security protocol."

One of the guards spoke into his mic, relaying the message.

Tension stretched between them during the nerve-racking standoff. Three guns against one. But it didn't take long for Chuck to show his face. A couple of minutes tops, and he was strolling downhill with an entourage of security guards.

"I'm here, Agent Striker," Chuck called from the illuminated path. "Would you and your cohort come out into the light for our little détente?"

"Move." Madeline nudged the guard she still held in front of her forward.

The other guards backed up slowly, stopping once they reached the walkway.

"Boys, lower your weapons," Chuck said, and they did as instructed.

Strolling closer, Chuck lifted his wrist to his mouth and whispered something. The lights along the path went from an amber glow to foot-ball-stadium wattage.

Madeline released the guard, stowed her gun in her purse and flashed her credentials in Chuck's face.

With a glib smile, Chuck proffered his hand. "Special Agent Striker. Chuck Albrecht. It's a pleasure to meet you."

Madeline glared at his outstretched hand with barely contained fury. "I wish I could say like-wise."

Chuck's gaze slid to Jackson and the weasel's eyes narrowed. "Jackson Rhodes? Is that a wig and fake mustache you're wearing?" He gestured to a guard, who promptly snatched the headpiece off Jackson. "Well, well, wonders never cease to amaze me. Did you put on this getup because you wanted to come tonight and see what my an-nouncement was about, but were afraid to face me?"

This jerk was full of perpetual hot air. "My daughter is missing, you son of a bitch, and I needed to see if you were behind it. But I didn't want the press to know that I was here. I don't want to make the situation worse for Emma."

Chuck held up the wig. Staring at it, he shiv-ered as if disgusted. "This explains why I couldn't find you after your invitation was scanned. De-spite a thorough search."

"What amazes me," Madeline said, "is that

your security personnel continued to fire their weapons at us after I identified myself clearly as a federal agent."

A smug smile tugged at one corner of Chuck's mouth. "How were my men supposed to know you were a legitimate FBI agent? Why would they believe you, considering the two of you were trespassing out here? I have every confidence that once they saw bona fide credentials they would have stopped shooting," he said, holding that evil grin. "Do you have a warrant, Special Agent Striker? Probable cause? Because if you don't, then your presence and search of this part of the premises is illegal. There's a little thing called the Fourth Amendment." He folded his arms. "My men are Russian mercenaries and have a strict 'shoot first and ask questions later' policy regarding trespassers. I don't mess around when it comes to my intellectual property, and no one dares mess with what's mine because of them. They had every right to open fire on intruders who broke into a restricted facility where I have tech worth billions. And I have every right to contact your supervisor and demand your badge. This stunt you two pulled is highly irregular, not to mention against the law."

Everything Chuck had said was true. Madeline didn't have a legal leg to stand on and what made it worse, Jackson had been the one to put her in that position.

"I believe your grievance is with me, Chuck," Jackson said, wanting to draw the slick bastard's line of fire away from Madeline. "I needed to know what you were working on."

"Curiosity killed the cat," Chuck said.

Clenching his jaw, Jackson gritted his teeth. "I had to see if what was inside that building was similar to my tech that was destroyed at my Duwamish site."

"Oh!" Chuck threw his head back and barked a laugh. "As if I might have been the one who blew up your facility and kidnapped your daughter. You thought *me* that desperate." He rolled his eyes. "Hopefully after tonight you've come to your senses and realized that I don't have to snatch your kid, destroy your tech and strong-arm you into resigning to beat you. Because I'm smarter and better than you and have two things you never will."

Jackson didn't ask the obvious question. He waited for the answer instead.

"Prodigious talent and ruthless ambition," Chuck said. "I was willing to put my own father out to pasture to get ahead since the old man was holding me back."

As if that was something to be proud of.

"And I have two things you don't," Jackson said. "A light touch and a tight grip. Step a little closer—I'll show you."

Chuck quirked an eyebrow and backed up.

"I'm signing a ten-billion-dollar contract with the DOD on Monday for my self-driving tanks. The only thing you have on me is about ten inches in height and those pretty-boy features. But I don't need that with my genius, money and talent. I truly do hope you find your daughter and take your job back at ETC. Do you want to know why?" A nasty grin spread across his face. "So I can have the satisfying pleasure of outperforming you. Every. Single. Quarter." Chuck had the nerve to wink at him. "Look, to show I'm sincere about hoping your daughter is returned safely to you, I'm going to have my guards show you the back way out, so you don't have to face the paparazzi without your disguise. I will not be held responsible for making things worse for Emma."

"Is this professional courtesy, one CEO to another?" Jackson asked.

More hearty laughter from Chuck grated on Jackson's nerves. "You're no longer a CEO. Remember? You resigned. Consider this a favor. Now you owe me, and the thought of you being in my debt puts a smile on my face."

The guards escorted them to the eastside exit, which was clear of snooping photographers, where Jackson's car met them.

On the drive back to his house, Madeline didn't look at him. Didn't say a single word. He could feel her justified anger, simmering below her calm exterior, but he decided it was best to wait to talk behind closed doors in the privacy of his home instead of giving the driver free entertainment.

Not that he was sure what to say.

The air in the car seethed with tension.

He was furious with himself. For not getting any closer to finding Emma's kidnapper and bringing her home. For his unethical plan backfiring. For endangering Madeline.

For not being able to erase from his mind that kiss he'd shared with her.

Suddenly, he could think of nothing else but the press of her lips against his mouth, her arms wrapped around him, her body molded to his, the wild heat flashing between them as natural and dangerous as lightning in a storm.

Shifting in the seat, he wished he could wipe out those images, forget the vivid sensations that had taken hold of him. But every time he glanced at her mouth, let his gaze trail down her bare arm, took in her scent with each inhale, they came flooding back.

The driver turned into the driveway and stopped the car. He and Madeline got out. Slammed the doors. Marched inside the house.

"Good old Chuck had it right, you know," she said before they'd made it out of the foyer. "What I did with you tonight was illegal. Do you have any idea what that could have meant to my career?"

He pressed on down the hall. "I know how much your job means to you. How important it is." He stalked into his bedroom, ripped off the fake mustache and shed his jacket. "I didn't want to make you complicit—that's why I asked you to wait for me at the main building. To protect you."

"It's my job to protect *you*. Not the other way around. Danger is a part of my career description, not recklessness. How could I wait for you at the main building while you ran off into the night to do only God knows what? You should have trusted me with the details of your plan. Given me a chance to think it through. But instead of working with me, like you promised, you went rogue. Again. And compromised me in the process."

"If had told you, you would've tried to stop me."

Her beautiful brown eyes blazed. "From trespassing? From breaking the law? Hell, yes."

Jackson stormed into the bathroom. Madeline followed

Turning on the faucet, he gathered his thoughts and tried to squelch the emotion raging inside him.

"There are rules for a reason," she said. "Limits and constraints serve a purpose. If we had found any evidence in that building, it would have been inadmissible."

"But any evidence, inadmissible or not, might

have led me to my daughter." He splashed water on his face and scrubbed the adhesive off his skin. "Sometimes you have to do the wrong thing for the right reason. If we hadn't, then we'd still be wasting time looking into Chuck. Spinning our wheels. Right?" He dragged a towel over his face and tossed it on the counter. Removing his tie, he brushed past her going back into his bedroom. "I had to get in there to see for myself. To be one hundred percent certain. Now we know he wasn't involved."

She was right on his heels. "If Albrecht decides to report me to the Bureau, I could be suspended."

He faced her, regretting that he'd put her at risk in any manner, professionally or physically. That had never been his intention.

"Fear is a powerful thing," he said. "Most people try to move away from fear, do what they can to alleviate it. Me? I lean into it, harness it so that I can make it work for me instead of against me. That's how I thrived in my father's house, with his expectations and high standards and efforts to tear me down so that he could rebuild me stronger. To this day, I still live my life leaning into the fear, heeding it, listening to it. Not running away from it."

Madeline stepped closer. "How does that have anything to do with what happened tonight?"

"The day Emma was kidnapped, I didn't listen

to it. This is one of my worst nightmares come to life. Losing Emma in plain sight. It's the reason I don't take her to amusement parks, malls, parades. I should've listened and brought Liane instead of worrying about my image. Since Emma has been gone, there's this knot in the pit of my stomach." A cold fist squeezing his gut sometimes to the point where he couldn't breathe. "Tonight, fear of missing an opportunity to discover the truth, to find Emma, drove me to do what I did. You're living proof that not all children who are taken are rescued. I couldn't choose not to take action when I had the power to do something. I'm sorry I dragged you into it."

"You made me look unprofessional out there," she said, soft and low, the furious wall she'd thrown up cracking and crumbling. "Worse, you made me *feel* like a fool. I trusted you, Jack."

The hurt he'd caused her was unmistakable, making him even more furious with himself, but it wasn't lost on him that the vulnerability she had dared show him was a precious gift.

He brushed his knuckles across her cheek, and she pulled her face away.

"Say that again," he whispered.

Confusion clouded her expression. "What?"

"My name. Say my name like that again." He touched her cheek once more, sliding his hand around, cupping the back of her neck.

This time, she didn't pull away.

As his grip on her tightened, she softened against him. She lifted a hand between them and put her palm to his chest. Whether to shove him back or bring him closer, he wasn't sure. He closed his fingers over her wrist, and she only stood there, staring at him, trembling.

"Jack," she said softly.

He lowered his mouth close to hers until an inch separated them and he held her gaze. "You're not a fool, Madeline, anything but."

The dark promise of a kiss hovered there, had the breath backing up in his lungs and his pulse throbbing hard and heavy.

There were times when he negotiated to get something. And there were times when he simply took. This was entirely different.

If they started, there would be no stopping. So in this, she had the power, and he was at her mercy. Despite how much he ached to abandon control and release the stress of the past few days, and just ravage.

"I'm bound by rules," she said, "and can't indulge myself in every reckless whim."

Were they still talking about AlbrechTech? "To hell with the rules, so long as you make it count when you break them."

Her mouth captured his then, her arms going around his neck, her fingers sliding into his hair. His kiss was ruthless, his mouth never leaving hers, but she was equally wild and hungry.

With nothing more than a kiss, she held him captive. This craving he had for her went far beyond chemistry. Beyond lust. Beyond his control.

Raw desire unlike anything he'd ever experienced surged through him. Blood pounded in his loins. He backed her to the wall beside the bed. She ripped his shirt open, sending popped buttons to the floor, and held him tighter.

This amazing woman had so much passion buried deep inside her and he wanted to unearth all of it.

She ran her hands over his chest, her fingers caressing, exploring. The brutal ache that had started deep inside him now swelled. He swallowed the groan that rose in his throat, but when Madeline whimpered, rubbing herself against him, the dam broke.

He wrenched the front of her dress down with one forceful tug and took in her beauty, her skin gleaming in the moonlight. "You're gorgeous. So gorgeous you take my breath away."

Cupping her breast, he reveled in the heavenly weight in his palm. Suckled a pert nipple. Slipped a hand through the convenient slit of her dress and found that hot button of nerves just beneath lace. Moaning, she arched against him. He tore off her panties and placed his palm firmly on the smooth mound between her thighs.

Her breath hissed out. "Yes. I want you."

He slid his fingers into her, his groan melding

with hers at the feel of her—wet, hot, tight. Desire coiled deeper inside him, snaking through him, gathering with the force of a storm. He wanted far more. Needed to be inside her like he needed air to breathe.

As if reading his mind, feeling the same hot desperation, she unbuckled his pants and lowered his zipper. Her warm hand closed around him, stroking the length of him. He yanked the hem of her dress up. She spread her thighs, giving him access that he capitalized on without a second of delay. He thrust his hips deeper, and she guided him home.

Everything melted away in the exquisite point of connection.

Their eyes locked on each other as the pleasure spread from the place where they were joined. It was then it struck him that they were still clothed except for the most intimate parts of their bodies.

He lifted her and in one fluid motion, turned and brought them down onto the bed.

Wild for her, he pressed his mouth to hers as he rocked into her, all his finesse evaporating. Her hands raced over him as she pumped her hips, driving him faster.

The need for release was fierce. All-consuming. Somewhere along the way, he lost his mind. Primitive instinct had taken over. His body was completely in charge. Nothing existed but Madeline, her sweet scent, the uncontrollable urge to plunge deeper, the ferocious need to satisfy the clawing hunger.

Madeline dug her nails into his back and clenched around him, coming undone beneath him.

With a guttural sound tearing from his lips, he quickly followed and the tension burst, setting him free.

BREATHLESS, MADELINE TRIED to recover as her skin rippled with the aftershocks of pleasure. Everything was a blur of heat and passion.

"Madeline." He rolled, bringing them onto their sides, and crushed her to him, pressing his damp face into the curve of her neck.

They stayed that way, chests heaving, clinging to each other until the haze cleared and reality dawned.

What on earth had she done?

Panic set in as she stilled.

All effort to maintain emotional distance had failed. Miserably. One minute they had been arguing. The next, he had touched her. Then they'd kissed, and desire had spread like a wildfire through tinder-dry brush.

That had been more than sex. A tangling of emotion with the physical. An assault of the senses that had stripped her bare. A release.

She hadn't thought, not for an instant. If she had, she would have heard that little voice inside her head telling her that she was breaking all the rules. She had crossed a personal Rubicon and there was no going back.

With every second that passed, she sensed him withdrawing, the connection between them slipping further away as his arms fell from her body and he lay on his back.

All the warmth receded into a marked chill.

"I'm sorry," she choked out, her voice so small she wasn't sure if he'd heard her.

But she glanced at him. Saw the soul-deep sadness etched on his face.

Her throat tightened. "That was a mistake," she muttered, needing to be the first one to say it. She tugged her dress up over her breasts and rearranged the rest of the fabric down over her hips, covering her legs. "I shouldn't have—"

"It takes two. This was more my fault than yours."

Fault. Corroboration this had been a mistake. Her heart pinched. "I'm sorry," she said again. "This was wrong."

"I don't regret it, but..."

She waited on pins and needles for him to finish. He didn't.

There really wasn't anything to say. She had taken an inappropriate step, lost control without thinking about any of the repercussions.

Goodness, they hadn't even used a condom.

"You don't have to say anything," she said, her

face growing hot from a different sort of heat. "I understand."

Jackson reached up, slipped his hand around the nape of her neck, bringing her closer, and kissed her softly. The stroke of his tongue into her mouth soothed the sting of his silence but didn't lessen her embarrassment.

"I do need to say it because you don't understand, Madeline. I barely understand it. You're everything I could want in a partner. Beautiful. Brilliant. Sexy. Independent. Full of guts."

*But…*that word and everything else he'd neglected to say echoed in her head. Loud and clear. He didn't need to explain his feelings or justify his actions. He was hurting, a parent stuck in one of the worst situations imaginable. While she was supposed to be the professional, his anchor getting him through this.

He looked into her eyes. "What happened between us wasn't wrong, but the timing *was*. I don't have the bandwidth to think about exploring a relationship. Not while Emma is missing. I feel guilty enough that I enjoyed myself with you just now."

Oh, God. That's what he thought. Jackson was fantastic when he wasn't infuriating her by going rogue. He was the kind of guy worth diving into a relationship with and taking a chance on to see if the fairy tale was possible, but she didn't want him to think that she was foolish enough to have any hope for something more between them.

The idea that he did set every internal rhythm haywire, had her heart and lungs battling for room inside her chest. "You needed comfort." Perhaps they both had. "That's all this was," she said, the words leaving her mouth in a rush. "A lovely distraction with no strings attached. No expectations. I promise."

He lifted up on his forearm and stared down at her. "So you took pity on me."

It would have been easier if the answer had been yes. "No. Adrenaline collided head-on with attraction." Electrifying attraction that neither of them could resist. "We slipped up. Gave in to a moment of weakness." One stupid, reckless moment. Nothing more.

"You're right. I couldn't stop myself from touching you." He brushed the back of his hand across her cheek and swallowed so hard it was audible. "Didn't want to because I needed you. I've never wanted anyone like that. I'm ashamed to admit that I still want you."

That made two of them. The ache deep inside her for him hadn't subsided either.

Madeline sat up. "I can call Nick or Dash and see if one of them is available to stay at the house with you tonight."

"I'd prefer if you didn't." The expression on

his face turned heartbreaking. "But I'd hate for things between us to become awkward."

He was worried this would further cloud her judgment, that she might hold some grudge against him.

"It won't become awkward," she said, her voice confident despite the truth of how she felt. "We can be adults about this."

He took her hand in his. "Stay. In here tonight. I don't want you to leave. I know that must sound selfish."

Madeline drew in a deep, heavy breath filled with the scent of him that made her throb with a yearning for more than she ever would admit.

"It sounds honest." Honesty she respected, even when it hurt, but if she stayed, they'd have sex again, this time without their clothes on. Having this conversation all over again in the bitter light of day would be ten times worse. She needed to scrape together whatever dignity she had left and get out of his bed. "I'll stay. In the guest room. Things need to go back exactly as they were. Good night." She pulled her hand away and scrambled down the hall as quickly as possible.

She shut the door of the guest room, leaned against it and squeezed her eyes closed. She could smell him on her, that intoxicating fragrance printed on her skin.

Her heart was still fluttering in her chest, aching though it shouldn't. She cursed her reaction to him. Her stupidity for getting too close.

A nice hot shower—or rather a cold one—and a good night's sleep would clear her head. In the morning, she'd tackle the day fully focused and get back on track.

No more distractions.

Chapter Twelve

To set the right tone, Jackson made breakfast while Madeline was in the bathroom getting ready. If they could share a meal, then everything would be all right.

He wasn't delusional in thinking that things between them would return to *normal*. What did that even mean? None of this was normal for him.

But he had a connection with Madeline, something deep, electric. An undeniable attraction. Last night, they had both acknowledged it and had acted upon it. If things were different, his life *normal*, then he could open himself to the possibility of a relationship. A prospect that appealed to him more than he had first grasped. He'd had a sleepless night thinking about her, smelling her on his sheets. Wanting the warmth of her next to him. The sound of her voice to keep him from spiraling down the rabbit hole.

And hours to hate himself for that desire while Emma was missing.

His chest ached at the realization that without this tragic chaos, he never would have even met Madeline.

Stealthy as a cat, Madeline walked into the kitchen, her face an unreadable mask.

His throat closed at the sight of her. Beautiful. Sophisticated. Intelligent eyes.

"Good morning," he said, setting down two plates of scrambled eggs, bacon and toast on the eat-in island.

"I'm heading out. I have a location on Samantha Dickson."

Now he had two reasons to get her to break bread with him. "Really, where?"

She watched him with very cool, very suspicious eyes. "An abandoned warehouse."

No address mentioned. Right.

He picked up the coffeepot. "As I recall, you need a hot cup of joe in the morning." He poured some of the steaming brew in a mug. "The time it would take you to go through a drive-through, you could spend drinking the coffee that is readily available this second." A vital point for any caffeine junkie to factor into consideration. "And have a quick bite to eat since I cooked."

"Jackson—"

"Please, Madeline."

Drawing a deep breath, she crossed the room and sat. "Thank you." She sipped her coffee.

The politeness felt a little too formal and stiff,

but he'd take it. "You're welcome." He sat beside her and began eating. "Dickson."

Before he could finish, she said, "No, you can't come."

"She's not on private property, is she? I believe you stated the warehouse is abandoned."

"It is."

"No danger of trespassing, then. What's the problem?"

"She may not talk if you're around."

"If I'm around, I guarantee she'll talk. The hothead won't be able to help herself. Samantha Dickson would never miss a chance to take a pro-verbial swing at me. In fact, get us in a room to-gether without her seeing you. If she has Emma or is responsible in any way, she'll rub it in my face because she knows it'd burn deeper than the acid they threw on my car."

Setting down her fork, Madeline looked at him, her eyes narrowing. "That might actually work."

"I'm full of good ideas." He hadn't made it to CEO for no reason, and then he remembered his resignation and a vicious sting followed.

She quirked her brow. "We only do this on one condition."

Anything she wanted, he'd do so as not to be excluded and stay at the tip of the spear with the investigation. "Name it."

"You wear a wire."

THE FBI VAN sat down the road from the warehouse that Dickson was holed up in, hidden behind another deserted building off Pier 30. Madeline parked the government SUV beside it. She and Jackson got out and walked to the van in tense silence, the same way they had driven around all morning.

Madeline had gone to the office earlier with Jackson and discussed the plan with Nick and Dash. Her ability to remain objective where Jackson was concerned was questionable at best. Luckily, her teammates had both agreed the idea was worth a shot.

Opening the van door, she gestured for Jackson to enter. They climbed in.

Nick and Dash were seated in front of the surveillance equipment ready to go.

"Get him set up." Dash handed her a kit containing the wire and slipped on headphones.

"Where's the pen?" Madeline asked. "The one with the listening device hidden inside. I thought we were using that."

"My fault," Nick said. "I grabbed the van, thinking there was one inside. The regular wire will work fine. It's not as if he's about to walk into a mobster's den where he's going to get a pat down." He stared at her, his brows drawing together. "Is there a problem I'm missing?"

Yes. "Nope. No problem." She opened the kit. "Jackson, can you lift your shirt for me?"

He took off his leather jacket and raised the hem of his cashmere pullover, exposing the broad expanse of his bare chest, the contours so defined in the bright light of day, or rather the glow of the equipment, that his sun-kissed skin gleamed as if polished.

Her heart flipped over at the sight. Biting the inside of her lip, she pulled out the first electrode, peeled off the plastic backing and stuck it to his torso. His muscles tensed, his gaze shooting to hers while a deep stab sank into her chest.

They had sworn this wouldn't be awkward, but it was because the attraction was there, simmering beneath the surface, burning in the shared glances, smoldering when they touched. It was torture.

Hurrying with the second electrode, she pressed it to his skin, struggling not to linger. She turned on the listening device and handed it to him. "Clip it on the inside of your waistband." Once he did, she said, "Try it out."

"Testing, one, two, three. Testing," Jackson said low.

Dash gave a thumbs-up.

"You're good to go," she said. "If you run into trouble of any sort, or need us to come in, give us a sign."

Jackson put on his jacket. "What kind?"

"Say you need a cigarette. Wish you had a smoke. Something along those lines."

"Since I don't smoke, there won't be any confusion, is that it?" he asked.

Madeline nodded. "Exactly."

"Okay," he said.

The tone of his voice, the look in his eye, made her wonder. Was this another mistake? Samantha Dickson was their last solid suspect, and Jackson was desperate for progress with the case. He would push for answers, take things right to the edge. Maybe even over the line. Provided he saw the line to begin with.

"This isn't a challenge—you don't need to prove you can handle it on your own," she said. "You will let us know if you need help, won't you?"

Those blue eyes shimmered with steely resolve. "Of course."

Why didn't she believe him?

Jackson put a hand on her shoulder and gave her a look that screamed, *I've got this.* "We'll know if they have Emma." He climbed out of the van and headed for the warehouse.

"You didn't sound too sure about this a second ago," Nick said. "Can he handle this?"

"We're sending him in to push buttons and get them talking. I have no doubt he'll achieve the objective." And that's what concerned her.

JACKSON STRODE THROUGH the front door of the warehouse, determined not to leave until he knew for certain whether the Red Right Hand were behind Emma's kidnapping.

Their suspects were evaporating one by one, and he didn't know how much more of this he could take. The waiting. The worrying. Twisting in the wind, not knowing who had taken his daughter or why. Someone wanted to punish him, and they were doing a good job.

A door opened on his far left. A group of five, maybe six twentysomethings, was gathered inside, sitting on mattresses, talking. One man with a scraggly beard Jackson recognized as a member of the Red Right Hand walked out and spotted him. "What are you doing in here?" The guy strolled up to him and took a closer look, his eyes narrowing. "Hey, I know you."

"I'm Jackson Rhodes and I'm here to see Samantha Dickson."

The guy snickered. "It's your funeral." He passed some old pallets and started up a steel staircase. "This way."

The abandoned warehouse was ten thousand square feet of decrepit space spread over two floors. The main level looked as though it had once been used for storage. Dust and mold filled the air. Sunlight streamed in through broken windows. Why anyone with choices for better options would want to stay there was lost on him.

Once they reached the catwalk, the guy said,

"Hang here." He knocked on the door of a former office, waited a second, then entered.

Before he closed it behind him, Jackson glimpsed the brown-haired Samantha canoodling with the red-haired Kane on a mattress in the center of the room.

When the door opened again, Samantha Dickson and Kane Tidwell strode out.

Samantha sported her perpetual wind-tousled look, face flushed, eyes narrowing, gearing up for a fight. "Well, if it isn't the Butcher of the American Dream in the flesh." She put her fists on her hips.

Kane stood beside her with his arms crossed over a wide, thick chest. He had a fleshy face and very small eyes. "You've got a pair of spuds on you. I'll give you that."

"Why do you stay here, living like squatters?" Jackson asked.

Samantha gave him a hateful smile. "As opposed to living in the biggest house, driving the most expensive car, burning electricity, wasting water, squandering resources and abusing Mother Earth until the future of the next generation is blacker than the oil extracted from her dying body?"

"It's not surprising that someone like you doesn't understand," Kane said. "Someone who doesn't care about his carbon footprint, global warming, fairness and equality, supporting

Americans by keeping jobs in America or basic decency like giving a little bit of those profits to charitable institutions."

"I sent those jobs overseas and *temporarily* stopped charitable donations to save ETC. A lot more people would've lost their jobs if not for my actions."

"As if that absolves you," Kane said. "Who the hell do you think you are?"

"He's someone who still hasn't learned his lesson," she said. Anger suited her. Samantha's face glowed as she stalked closer.

"You think the Red Right Hand is capable of teaching it to me?" Jackson asked.

Samantha's smile spread. "No job. No fancy project. No kid. But I think you still have plenty left to lose. And once you hurt enough, your eyes will open. We're the perfect group to give you an awakening."

"Get the others," Kane said to his pal. "Trash his car. Make sure he has to walk home."

Mr. Scraggly Beard hustled past them across the catwalk and hurried down the steps.

"That's if we let him leave," Samantha said.

"You want to make me disappear like you did with my daughter?" Jackson asked, his temperature rising.

Confusion clouded Samantha's eyes.

But Kane didn't so much as blink.

The rest of their gang ran outside carrying pipes and pieces of wood.

They were in for a surprise.

"Our mission in life," Kane said, "is to make sure that people like you get exactly what you deserve. Balance the scales of justice."

"You call snatching my child justice?" Jackson demanded. "I call it reprehensible. Evil."

Kane stepped closer, putting them within arm's reach. "You don't deserve to have a child." He poked Jackson's chest. "Raising a mini you to help destroy the world and pick its bones clean."

"You shouldn't have put your hands on me," Jackson said, making it clear to those listening in the van that what happened next wasn't his fault.

He snatched the man's wrist and twisted his arm hard. Pressing his free hand into Kane's back, Jackson pushed the man's torso until it was parallel to the ground while wrenching his captured arm up. The pressure on the twerked shoulder was enough to elicit a shriek from Kane.

The others ran back into the warehouse at the same time. "There's no car out front." They gasped and made a beeline for the stairs.

"Get off him!" Samantha said. "Let him go." She pounded her fists on Jackson's back.

"Where's my daughter?" Jackson shoved down harder on Kane, making him scream in pain. "Let her go and I let him go."

"We don't have your stupid kid!" Samantha

said. "We're not like you. We don't take advantage of the innocent."

"What do you say?" Jackson asked Kane. "Huh? Did you have anything to do with her kidnapping?"

Scraggly Beard and the others stormed down the catwalk toward them, holding up their pipes and hunks of wood.

"No!" Kane said.

"Sure?" Jackson pressed down.

"I swear!" Kane said. "We don't kidnap children. Not even the spawn of monsters."

Jackson believed them. He would've let Kane go, would've yelled for a cigarette, but it was too late, and everything unraveled too fast.

Scraggly Beard swung the pipe. So Jackson swung Kane, lowering the seized wrist and forcing Kane's body up to take the blow.

Metal connected with bone. Blood sprayed through the air from Kane's mouth.

Horror widened Scraggly Beard's eyes at his mistake. Samantha gave a spine-chilling scream.

The others stormed forward, brandishing their weapons.

Since letting go would be to his own detriment, Jackson held on to Kane, making sure he took more hits than Jackson received.

"FBI!" Nick said, racing in through the door.

"Stop!" Madeline's voice came next. "Put your hands in the air!"

Once again, too late.

A pipe slammed into Jackson's ribs and pain exploded through his side. The force of the blow knocked him back against the railing. Momentum carried him over the side of the catwalk. And still he held on to Kane, taking the man with him.

Chapter Thirteen

Two ambulances and four squad cars were on the scene. The entire Red Right Hand was already wanted for crimes committed last night: vandalism, for spray-painting graffiti on the Albrech-Tech building, and destruction of property, for smashing the windows of Chuck's car. Now a couple of them would also face assault charges.

Kane Tidwell was loaded in an ambulance.

"Please let me go to the hospital with him," Samantha begged as she was handcuffed and put into the back of a police cruiser.

Madeline stepped into the back of the other ambulance, where Jackson lay on a gurney. She was grateful he was conscious and had the strength to argue with the EMT.

"I'm fine," Jackson said. "Kane broke my fall. Going to the hospital isn't necessary."

"Definitely a couple of broken ribs and a possible concussion," the EMT said.

Sheer panic had flooded her when Jackson fell

from the catwalk. It had happened in slow motion. She hadn't been able to breathe, move; it had been as if her heart had stopped.

The funny thing was, when he opened his eyes and spoke, she had one overwhelming thought. *Thank God I didn't lose him.*

She'd had to remind herself that he wasn't hers. Once this case was over, they'd go their separate ways.

Still, Madeline found herself taking his hand before she realized she'd broken her rule and was touching him, and by then she didn't want to let go of him. "You're going to the hospital."

"I need to be out there, looking for Emma. I have to find her." His face filled with so much despair that Madeline's heart broke. "If the Red Right Hand didn't take her, then who did?"

Since she had no answer to give him, she frowned down at their joined hands. The need to find out who was behind this and save Emma was like a fire burning in her gut, spurring her on. Not to give up. Never.

She'd exhaust every possibility, chase down each lead. But she'd never stop trying.

Her phone rang. She pulled her hand from his and answered. "Yeah, Striker."

"It's Liam. I was going to update the file, but thought it was better to tell you."

"One sec." She glanced at the EMT. "Could you give us a minute, before you take him to the hospital?" After the woman nodded and hopped out, Madeline waved Dash and Nick over and put the call on speaker. "Go ahead, Liam. I have the others here along with Jackson."

"Some of the newspapers go back three years," Liam said.

"Three?" Madeline asked. "Are you sure?"

"Positive. I was only able to find two articles that were related to ETC and one also mentioned Jackson."

"What were they about?" Dash asked.

"One was about the video game department and the other was an obituary for a former ETC employee. The article talked about Jackson cutting the division and a big sale of the games."

"Did you have a bunch of angry engineers and designers?" Nick asked.

Jackson shook his head. "The one department at ETC that shouldn't have a grievance with me was Games. I made all of them rich. Except for one guy. Lou Jenkins. He received the smallest severance package, but it was still generous. I heard he rebounded and is thriving at a new company. This has to be a coincidence."

"Maybe," Madeline said. "But you do this job long enough and you stop believing in coincidences. You weren't really involved with the day to day of the video games department, were you?" she asked, thinking there might have been things going on in the office that he hadn't been aware of.

"I wasn't in the trenches with my people," Jackson said, "but I tried to keep my finger on the pulse of things. I have, had, an open-door policy."

"Who was the head of the video games department?" Madeline asked.

"Dennis Garcia," Jackson said. "A good guy. Retired now. I've had him to the house for dinner once or twice."

"What about the obit, Liam?" Madeline asked. "Who was it for?"

"Theon Lasiter, but it doesn't say what department he worked in."

Jackson sat up and winced. "You're right. It's not coincidence. Theon worked for me, in Games. But I don't understand how it could be related to Emma's kidnapping."

"How did Theon Lasiter die?" Dash asked.

Jackson shrugged. "I didn't even know he was dead. He walked away from ETC with the biggest check of all."

"There's a correlation with the games department," Madeline said. "We just have to find it. I should sit down with Garcia and talk with him. See what we're missing."

"I'll track down Lou Jenkins," Nick said.

Dash tilted his head, like he was thinking. "I'll go back to the office and see what I can find on

Lasiter's death. Liam, keep plugging away at the articles."

"Where does Garcia live?" Madeline asked Jackson, wondering how long the drive would be.

"I can get you the address from HR." He reached into his pocket to take out his phone and groaned in pain. "I believe his house is in Olympic Manor."

Probably a thirty-minute drive, depending on traffic. "I'll pay him a visit. Talk to him in person," Madeline said. "No stone left unturned. And you are going to the hospital."

Madeline's estimation had been correct. After Jackson got her the address, it took her twenty-eight minutes before she parked in front of the Tudor-style house in Olympic Manor and made her way up the front steps. She knocked and waited.

The door opened. A man stood slightly taller than her on the other side of the threshold. With a round face and kind eyes, he smiled. "Hello."

She held up her badge. "I'm Special Agent Madeline Striker. Are you Dennis Garcia, the former chief of the gaming department at Emerald Technology Corp?"

"Yes, I am. What can I do for you?"

"I'd like to ask you some questions that might help us with the kidnapping of Emma Rhodes, the six-year-old daughter of Jackson Rhodes."

He rocked back. "I heard about that, but I don't understand how I can be of any help."

"Do you mind if I come in?" Madeline asked.

"Certainly." He opened the door wide, letting her in. "Would you care for something to drink?"

"A glass of water, please," she said, her throat parched.

"We can speak in the kitchen, if that's all right."

They walked through the tidy home, passing the living room, dining room, and Madeline sat at the small bistro-style table by the window.

Garcia handed her a bottle of water from the fridge and grabbed a can of soda for himself.

She opened the bottle and chugged some of the cool water. "I'm going to record this conversation, if you don't mind."

"Not at all. Go ahead."

She took the recorder from her pocket and set it on the table. "How would you describe the layoff of the games department at ETC?"

"In a word, profitable."

"Did you agree with Jackson Rhodes's decision to sell off the games and dismantle your department?"

Garcia opened his Coke. "Didn't matter if I agreed. I understood why it had to happen. Made complete sense. Allowed me to pay for this house in cash and have a comfortable retirement."

"But it wasn't profitable for everyone, was it?

What about Lou Jenkins? Was he angry when he didn't receive a big fat check?"

Garcia chuckled. "Lou was grateful he walked away with as much as he did. He was at the bottom of the pack and knew it. Got a new position at another company. As an animator. I see him from time to time. He's much happier. Doing really well for himself."

"Do you recall another employee who worked under you—Theon Lasiter?"

His eyebrows shot up. "How could I ever forget?"

"Can you tell me about him?"

"Theon was special. Gifted, I mean. Singular in his vision. It took him a while to find his niche when he first started working at ETC. None of the games he developed had really taken off. But he had an interesting background that I thought he could use as inspiration for a game."

"Interesting in what way?"

"He grew up in a survivalist community. Real hard-core. Almost cultlike if you ask me."

"You mean like preppers?" Madeline asked.

Garcia chuckled. "I once foolishly thought they were the same thing, too, until Theon schooled me. There are some significant differences. Preppers and survivalists both plan and prepare for that doomsday scenario. A megadisaster. But how they prepare is where they diverge. One group is focused on stockpiling and the other on developing a finely honed skill set."

"So I take it, the preppers are the ones loading up their shelves with canned goods, water, powdered milk, that sort of thing."

Nodding, Garcia opened his soda. "That's about right."

"What type of skill set does the survivalist cultivate?"

"Instead of stockpiling massive amounts like preppers, survivalists become experts at fishing, snaring, foraging, hunting. They're the ones with the guns, make no mistake about that."

She couldn't help but think about the fire on Jackson's lawn. How tree resin was the secret weapon for surviving in the wilderness. "Survivalists are focused on building up an arsenal?"

"No, no. They like to stay light on their feet." Garcia sipped his soda. "They'll have a couple of guns in a bug-out bag and will train to be crack shots, but they'll have knives, too. Think of it like this, you and I have GEICO—they have body armor. Instead of building a garden, they're creating booby traps, making homemade bombs, that sort of thing. Defense and offense are key to survivalists. Not stockpiling."

A homemade bomb had been used to blow up the Duwamish site. Forensics confirmed tree resin had been the accelerant. The same compound used in the fire on Jackson's front lawn.

"Where was the survivalist group based that Theon grew up in?"

"Loon Lake. On the east side of the state. Four or five hours from here."

Madeline logged the place, updating the shared document, though it seemed too far away for the kidnapper. Seemed more likely that Emma's abductor was within an easy drive of Jackson.

"Tell me about the game he created," she said.

"It's called Survivalist Zone. Apocalypse scenario. Players build a zone, establish a home, and then they have to protect it. Sometimes a player will need to attack another player's position to claim vital resources. The game was an instant hit. But it still had a lot of untapped potential. Theon wanted to make the next version more elaborate and complicated. Jackson was still overseeing the department at the time and supported Theon when the kid wanted to create a real-life mock-up, complete with booby traps and everything. ETC had some land that they weren't using and gave him the green light. His older sister even came out to help him make it as realistic as possible. She never even asked for any name recognition or credit."

"Sister?" A shiver raced down her spine. "What was her name?"

"Chloe. Chloe Lasiter."

Madeline sent a red alert to the team with the

name. She wanted Dash digging into the sister as soon as possible.

"She was devoted to Theon," Garcia said. "When the video game was sold and our department was cut, I think she was as devastated as her brother."

"If the game was successful, why was it sold?"

"That's the *reason* it was sold. Because it was successful."

"I'm not tracking the logic," Madeline said. "Why sell a game that's making a solid profit?"

"Theon's game was computer based. Had a strong cult following. Wildly popular. It's an open world and users contribute content, making the game grow. Generated revenue and profits. Brought in millions. Double digits. But Jackson sold it to a company who already had a foothold with video game consoles. The other company could expand the game to their consoles and their dedicated app store. And make an even bigger profit."

"How much did the intellectual property sell for?"

"Two. Point. Five. Billion."

Madeline reeled back. "Goodness."

"Brilliant move on Jackson's part." Garcia nodded with a look of awe twinkling in his eyes. "He did the same with the other moneymaking video games in the department. It was simply more profitable for ETC to sell. But Survivalist

Zone was by far the biggest. Theon and the others walked away millionaires. Like me."

"Then what was the problem?" Madeline asked. It sounded as if the entire department should've been kicking up their heels and moving on to greener pastures. "Why wasn't Theon happy about the sale even if it meant the loss of his own department?"

"The problem was Theon didn't care about the money. He wanted to remain affiliated with the game and future developments. But the buyer said no. They wanted to take the game in their own direction. Theon was crushed. He had poured his heart and soul into that game. Had spent so much time and energy working on it that his wife divorced him when it was in the beta stage. All he had left was that game. It was his baby. His brainchild," he said, putting pieces of the puzzle together for Madeline. "And when what he cared about most was taken from him, he lost it. Cracked. Spiraled into a dark depression. Then I heard he killed himself. So sad. He left Chloe all his money. Fifteen million."

She let out a low sound of surprise.

"Sounds like a lot. To most people it is, more than they'd see in a lifetime. But when you think about it, fifteen mil was only one percent of the profit Jackson and ETC made from the sale. Not that the cash mattered to survivalists like Theon and Chloe. I saw her at the funeral. She was heartbroken. She blamed ETC for his death. Blamed Jackson."

Chloe Lasiter was behind this. Madeline knew it deep in her heart. "Can you describe what Chloe looks like?" Madeline asked, urgency propelling her.

Garcia shrugged. "She's about thirty, maybe thirty-two by now. Fair skinned. Long chestnut brown hair. Hazel eyes like Theon. On the slim side but not petite. She was athletic and on the taller side."

The description didn't match any of their suspects. But it fit the profile for the unsub and gave a strong personal motive to target Jackson that was tied directly to ETC business.

"Those two put so much into the development of that game," Garcia said again, his eyes looking haunted. "You know ETC still has the site where they built their real-world mock-up. The company never tore it down. Probably forgot about it."

"Where is it? I'd like to check it out for myself." Walking around the site and seeing what Theon had created with his sister might be the best way for Madeline to get inside Chloe's head. Understand what she was truly capable of and how far she might be willing to go for revenge.

Garcia wrote down the location for her since it was more a set of directions than an actual address.

"Going out there will shed light on what inspired the game. Reflects the darkness that was in their heads, much more than the video game would. Though that Survivalist Zone can get pretty dark with people stealing resources and killing each other. It's a bit of a drive, about an hour outside of the city up in the mountains. But once you see the site, it'll have you praying that you never come up against a survivalist."

AN ELECTRIC HUM from Dash's computer system purred in the air just beneath the clatter of his frantic typing on the keyboard. Since he'd gotten Madeline's alert, Dash had been parked behind his desk at BAU headquarters, feverishly trying to dig up whatever he could on Chloe Lasiter, including a picture.

It was like she was a ghost. No social media presence. No property records. No utility bills.

Maybe her brother had been more active and had left a digital footprint.

Dash redirected his search to Theon Lasiter. Once again, no Facebook, no Instagram, no Snapchat. No old property records either.

But all serious gamers were on Twitch—a livestreaming platform tailored for that crowd—and Discord, which was a means for people to easily communicate while playing PC games together.

Already his fingers were darting across the

keys. The screens shuddered and flickered as he typed faster.

Sure enough, Theon and Chloe had profiles on both sites. No pictures. Only avatars.

Dash glanced at his second monitor, which showed the results of the search on Theon. There was a magazine article featuring Theon as the Game Awards winner for Content Creator of the Year three years ago. Clicking on the link, he scrolled through the article that touted Theon as someone to watch over the next decade. Theon had been quoted stating he was thrilled his sister had finally moved to Seattle and they were about to close on a house they'd bought together.

That meant there was a property in one or both their names. Maybe under an LLC—limited liability company—for privacy since he had been gaining a bit of fame in the industry.

Scrolling a little further, Dash came to a picture of Theon holding the Game Award up in one hand, his arm slung over the shoulder of a young woman, with their temples pressed together. The caption listed the smiling brunette as Chloe Lasiter.

She looked so familiar, but he couldn't place her. Was it the hair?

Dash zoomed in, two clicks, and his heart slammed against his rib cage as he stared at the picture.

"Holy hell."

He knew exactly who that was. Without a doubt. He'd done a background check on her personally, and hadn't found any red flags under the alias she'd used. How was that possible?

Reaching for the phone to call Madeline, he reconsidered. Before Dash called her, he needed to get Liam to help him do a deep dive and cull as much useful information on this woman as they could to find the Rhodes kid fast. Madeline was going to have a ton of questions for him, and he had better be prepared with answers.

Dialing Liam to save himself the time of running down the hall, he glanced back at the woman's face on his screen.

At the kidnapper.

Liane Strothe.

Chapter Fourteen

Jackson answered his phone, relieved it was a call from Madeline and not another text message designed to torture him.

"Are you okay?" Madeline asked.

Shifting in the seat in the back of his Uber, he stifled a groan. "Yeah. I'm fine. No concussion. Only a couple of broken ribs."

"Only? You're lucky a lung wasn't punctured in the fight."

"Tidwell looks worse." That was the truth.

"Are they holding you the night for observation?"

"They checked me out and an Uber is dropping me off at home as we speak." His Uber parked in front of his house instead of in the driveway.

"The doctor checked you out," Madeline said, "or did you take it upon yourself to simply leave?"

"Same difference." Jackson tipped the driver from the app on his phone and got out beside his mailbox. It had been a few days since he had last checked it. The thought hadn't even occurred to him with everything else going on. He opened the mailbox and grabbed the bundle of envelopes inside. "Did you turn up anything with Dennis?"

Walking up the drive, he sifted through the junk mail.

"Actually, I think I did," Madeline said. "I believe this might all be centered around Theon Lasiter and his suicide."

Jackson staggered to a halt. "Theon killed himself?" He was a bright kid, talented. A real wunderkind who had loads of potential. It was such a shame. "You know his revamped version of Survivalist Zone was an overnight success. Thanks to him, we made a large enough profit from the sale of his game that I was able to…" His stomach turned to ice. He hadn't seen it before, but the link solidified clearly for him.

"What were you going say?"

"I was able to fund my pet project at Duwamish. Moving forward on the stealth technology wouldn't have been possible without that sale." The ice spread up into his chest.

"My gut was right. This is about Theon."

This still didn't add up. Something else was missing. "But Theon is dead. So who took Emma?"

"I believe it was his sister, Chloe. Did you ever meet her?"

Jackson stepped onto his porch. "No. I almost did once. She attended the Game Awards with him. I was supposed to go to show my support, but Emma had a fever that night. I stayed home with her."

"Theon's sister worked with him on Survivalist Zone," Madeline said. "She helped him create the real-world mock-up to make the video game more intense and realistic. I'm headed out there now to take a look. I think seeing the place might give me better insight into who Chloe is and how her mind works since she helped her brother design it."

"Why don't you swing by here and we can go together?" Jackson suggested. He knew the lay of the land, more or less, and could show her around while making sure she didn't get hurt.

"You should rest. Besides, I've already passed Madison Park. I'm about to get off the 520 and hit the 405."

No one should go out there alone. Jackson had been to the site when construction had first started and once it had been completed. Theon had let his imagination run wild with the concept, and the end result was somewhat terrifying. Apparently, his sister had helped.

Two dark minds were better than one.

"Be careful," Jackson said. "You could get a flat tire on the road alone leading into the site.

Pretty rocky terrain from what I recall and the place itself is quite dangerous. We put a fence up around the three-acre property to keep hikers from wandering in, getting injured and filing a lawsuit. You'll need a code to access it. Come and pick me up and I'll give it to you."

"There's no sense wasting time doubling back. What's the code?" The firm tone in Madeline's voice made clear that she would brook no argument.

He sighed with resignation. "If Andrew never changed it, and I doubt that he'd take enough interest to bother, then it should be 75688."

Madeline's line beeped. "Jackson, I've got another call. From Dash. Might be an update with information on Chloe. Listen, try to get some rest. Once I know something concrete, I'll call or come by."

"Stay safe." He hung up.

Closing the door behind him, he dropped the mail onto the foyer table. A flyer slipped to the floor. At the top of the pile on the table was an envelope with his name spelled out in letters meticulously cut from newspapers and magazines.

Jackson ripped open the envelope and pulled out a note. The message, created with the same type of letters from periodicals, was another sucker punch to his soul.

Get rid of the FBI. No police.
Then I will tell you where to meet. Alone.
Midnight.
Do it if you ever want to see your daughter again.

MADELINE DISCONNECTED THE call with Jackson and clicked over to the other line on Bluetooth. "Please tell me you found something."

"I hit pay dirt," Dash said. "Chloe Lasiter is Liane Strothe."

Madeline's heart stuttered. *Oh, my God.* "The nanny?" They'd had her and let her go.

"Yep. I'm sending you a picture now of Theon and Chloe together."

Her phone buzzed. She tapped the message, bringing up the photo and zoomed in. Sure enough. Chloe had long, dark hair just as Dennis Garcia had described and didn't wear glasses, but the eyes, the nose, everything else was the same. *Liane.*

Madeline shook her head, but the shock didn't dampen. How had she not connected the dots and realized? Chloe… Liane had been right in front of her.

"She's been with Jackson and Emma for almost two years," Madeline said. Two years of scheming and planning, getting to know Jackson and what made him tick, to figure out the nastiest way possible to hurt him.

Jackson had told Madeline that his worst nightmare had been to lose Emma in plain sight. In front of him. Rather than easily snatching the girl at any time, Liane had strategized how to make that nightmare a reality that had left Jackson swamped with guilt.

"A long time, I know," Dash said. "Turns out that Chloe Lasiter bought the nanny agency that Jackson used. I spoke with the placement coordinator. She claims she's never met Lasiter in person, but that Chloe was the one who hired Liane. Guess when? One week before Jackson's previous nanny had a car accident that forced her to quit."

She hired her own alter ego, then took out the caregiver in order to replace her. That was creepy.

The degree of deception Liane had gotten away with was staggering. It unnerved Madeline, chilling her to the marrow. The commitment. The patience. The high level of manipulation and organization. Liane was a psychopath. Calculating and carefully plotting each move, using focused aggression in a planned-out manner to get what she wanted.

No wonder Liane had been a mile ahead of them. She'd had two years to devise every step.

"But she had an alibi." Madeline thought about all the ways she'd been diverted from looking deeper into the woman as a suspect. "You saw it yourself. She was at the movie theater for three and half hours."

"We watched the footage again. During the playback we saw how she did it. After she hit the concession stand and entered the theater, she changed her top. Actually she put on a black hoodie and removed her wig and glasses. It must've been hidden in the backpack. We caught it this time because of her shoes. The same Converse sneakers. When we zoomed in, it was her. Not only that, but there's also more. Once I confirmed it was her, I checked the cinema's parking lot footage. She drove the black Ford Transit to the movies. That means—"

"Emma had been in the back of the van at the time."

"Liane parked at the far end of the lot away from any other cars," Dash said. "If the kid had been in there, tied up and gagged, no one would've heard her."

Madeline's stomach churned into a knot. "The last text Jackson received from her came through while she was sitting across from me in the interview room. How did she pull that off?"

"She must have used a timed app to send the message. Deliberately synced it to happen while she was at the office to throw us again," he said. "And you're not going to believe this. The name Liane Strothe is an anagram for Theon Lasiter. It's almost as if she wanted Jackson to figure it out. She's been right in front of us the whole time. We just didn't have all the pieces to see it."

Questions cascaded through Madeline's head in a deluge. "What about the background check you ran on her?"

"Looks like she must've paid a pretty penny for the extensive identity she had created. It was professional. Done by the best of the best. Detailed to look and feel real. The data trail went all the way to childhood medical records."

An identity invented and two years invested to get back at Jackson. The knot in her stomach tightened. This whole time they had been playing the wrong game. They didn't even know who the hell Chloe Lasiter was.

But Madeline was going to find out.

"We got an address for Lasiter. Purchased under an LLC Theon had formed with her for privacy," Dash said. "She owns a house on the north side of town. Near Sand Point." He rattled off the address. "Isolated area located far from any other homes. It's likely she's holding the girl in her garage or basement. Nick and I are headed there now with the police to search the place."

That would be easier said than done.

"If you're still in Olympic Manor, you've got time to meet us for the raid."

"I'm not." She was on the opposite side of Lake Washington. "Listen, Chloe Lasiter has been the epitome of careful, organized. You guys need to take extra precautions. The woman is an expert at bomb making and booby traps. She won't just let you waltz in and take Emma. She'll defend the house."

"Lasiter never thought we'd figure out her real identity. That's what she considers to be her safe house. Still, we're playing it by the book. Nick coordinated with the bomb unit and SWAT. We're all en route together. Every precaution that can be taken is. Seriously, don't…worry… the kid…be there," he said, breaking up. "…got this…covered."

If he was right and they took Liane by surprise, things could still go wrong. Getting caught wasn't part of her plan and she certainly wasn't finished with Jackson. No telling what else she had in store for him, and there weren't going to be any exceptions regarding the target of her vengeance. Liane had gotten a taste of power, enjoyed the sweetness of her revenge and wasn't ready to give that up. Being forced to deviate from her plan would make her panic.

Panic was a potent thing. Highly volatile like tree resin. It had the power to change a person. Robbed them of rational thought. Thus far, Liane hadn't killed anyone, but Madeline knew all too well that panic could turn a person into a murderer. All that was needed was the equivalent of a lit match.

Madeline clenched the steering wheel, her

palms growing sweaty. "How far out are you?" she asked.

"We'll be…in fifteen minutes."

Madeline factored the time it would take her to turn around and drive clear across town to meet them. Forty minutes at best. "I'm almost at the Survivalist Zone site," she said, slowing down on the rocky road. "Be there in ten minutes." That was her best guess off the time estimate Dennis had given her since there was no address to load in the GPS. "I still want to check it out." No point in wasting the drive. "Call me as soon as you search the place and let me know what you find, one way or the other."

"Hello? Hello? Madeline, I…can't—"

The signal cut out.

Great. She checked her phone. No bars. She looked around beyond the trees to the hills and mountains of the valley she was in. The terrain must be interfering with the cell phone signal.

She passed an ETC sign warning against trespassers and to only enter the area at your own risk.

A QUARTER OF a mile from the Lasiter house, Nick stopped the vehicle, and everyone else pulled over behind him. It took two minutes to huddle up. The best route of approach was through the woods where the suspect wouldn't see them coming. She lived off the beaten path with the closest neighbor half a mile down the road.

"The suspect should be considered armed and dangerous," Nick said to the team of law enforcement assembled. "She's proficient in homemade explosives and setting booby traps. SWAT will check the rear entrance, which is the target ingress point, for any explosive devices. If they find something, the bomb squad will take care of it. Once inside, we need to move quickly but cautiously. Sharp eyes as you clear rooms because we don't know if there might be any nasty surprises waiting for us. Remember, the suspect is holding a six-year-old girl captive in a room with no windows, a garage or a basement. Our number-one goal is to get the hostage out unharmed."

They needed to bring this case to a close. The right way. No shots fired and no casualties was preferred.

Everyone acknowledged the directives.

Nick's adrenaline surged as he drew his service weapon and gave the signal for the team to move out.

They crept through the woods, silent and alert. It was a good thing there were no neighbors in the vicinity. One less thing to contend with. One less factor to cause a complication that could affect the outcome.

Once they made it to the edge of the wood

line, Nick whispered into comms, "Hold. Everyone hold."

The house was a two-bedroom ranch style. Fifteen hundred square feet. Drawn curtains covered the windows, blocking a view of the interior.

Nick watched for a minute while he slipped a tactical light on the rail of his Glock. No sign of movement inside, no shadows, no lights, no rustling of the curtains. Then he gave the hand signal for SWAT to advance.

The four-man team hustled up to the rear door, taking their positions. Using their equipment and a tactical under-door camera, two men checked the entrance for explosives. Everyone else waited, tense and watchful. A quick thumbs-up indicated it was all clear. This was it. The other two guys swung forward with a battering ram.

There was nothing for Nick to do besides prepare to enter, steadying his nerves, which were the byproduct of adrenaline. Being wired and impatient served nobody. He smoothed out emotions like ice under a Zamboni and then he was ready to rock and roll.

The ones holding the battering ram had an internal count bred from practice—fast, efficient, fluid. On the third swing they breached the door.

Boom! The force brought the door down, tearing it from its hinges.

Nick and Dash were already on the move.

They swept inside the house, going in a different direction from SWAT.

The interior was dimly lit with no natural light filtering in. Nick switched on the flashlight he had attached to his weapon. Dash did the same.

The garage was on the west side of the house, where Nick and Dash were headed.

Over comms, the others reported in as they cleared rooms. No kid. No Chloe. Nothing.

At the garage door, Nick and Dash positioned themselves on either side of the frame with their backs to the wall. Any potential explosive devices were more likely to have been placed at an exterior door or window. They exchanged a glance and Nick nodded, giving the go-ahead.

Dash tried the doorknob. It would be quieter and easier if it was unlocked. The knob turned. He swung the door open and pulled back in case of any incoming gunfire.

With his gun at the ready, Nick was the first through the door. Dash followed in.

The garage was empty, and the walls were bare. There were no signs that anyone had been held hostage.

Reporting in over the radio, Nick moved back toward the center of the house.

One of the SWAT guys came up to him in the kitchen. "No basement and no attic. But we found something you'll want to see."

Nick followed him into the living room.

One half of the main wall was covered in newspaper articles. Nick swept his flashlight over the headlines and read them. Some Liam had found and discussed. Others were about the success of the Survivalist Zone video game, Theon Lasiter winning an award, Jackson selling the games and cutting the department to make billions in profit. Theon Lasiter's suicide. Jackson braving a new frontier for ETC.

Nick and Dash shared a look, then they moved down to the other side of the wall.

A picture of Jackson Rhodes with a red *X* drawn over his face was front and center at the middle of a web. Chloe had drawn lines to the connections. The nanny agency. The Duwamish site. Emma Rhodes. Maybe *web* wasn't the right word. It was a labyrinth of pain and misery that she had plotted out. All of it led to one final piece. The Survivalist Zone site—the image looked exactly like the cover of the video game.

"That's where she's holding Emma," Dash said.

"Maybe that's her endgame, where she wants to finish it. So that Jackson will know why. I mean, none of this means anything unless Jackson understands what he did wrong in her mind and why he's being punished."

"Then why hasn't she lured him out there already?" Dash asked.

Nick shrugged, thinking it through. "She hasn't·

had the chance. Madeline has been with him the entire time. Chloe needs him alone and unmonitored."

Dash looked at him, his eyes widening with concern. "But Madeline is on her way out there now."

Someone flicked on the light switch.

There was a popping sound. Then electricity hissed and crackled. The smell of pine and burning wires permeated the air.

"Move! It's rigged!" someone else yelled. "Go! Go!"

Nick and Dash bolted for the back door. But SWAT jumped through windows. Their exit was faster, smarter. Nick cut to the right, heading for the closest window. Raising his arm to shield his face, he dived through the pane of glass and rolled onto the grass. Dash leaped through next, landing beside him, just as the bomb went off.

Chapter Fifteen

Madeline stopped at the locked gate to the Survivalist Zone mock-up. In between the six-foot-high bars, she saw a cabin. One story with a chimney. Looked like any other cozy cabin. Part of her expected to see some kind of obstacle course, but according to Dennis Garcia the point was that intruders weren't meant to see the defenses.

She punched in the code Jackson had given her and it worked.

Pushing the gate open, she looked around at the lush evergreens, listened to the wind whispering through the soft needles. The forest was serene.

She drove through, leaving the gate open, and parked a few feet from the cabin.

At the small porch, she checked for hidden traps before stepping up on it. The doorknob twisted, and she pushed the door in, staying outside in case something had been triggered.

But there was nothing. She entered, one step at a time, looking and listening as she went.

With a quick glance around the open space, Madeline determined that no one was inside, though someone had been. The unmade cast-iron bed had been occupied recently. She put her hand to the side of a thermos on the table. It was warm.

Pushing her jacket behind the holster on her hip, she put her hand on her weapon.

The cabin had windows with no curtains, which let in plenty of natural light. The floor and walls were wood. Bare, not plastered with newspaper. Except for one.

Madeline crossed the room. On the wall, near the top, was a picture of Theon, smiling, holding a copy of his video game in one hand and in the other an award—a statuette that resembled the *Winged Victory of Samothrace* but with a head. Below the photo was a list of actions Jackson had taken that led to the obituary of Theon Lasiter. Madeline glanced over at a metal chair that was bolted to the floor and faced the wall.

Was the chair meant for Jackson?

Maybe Chloe wanted to draw Jackson here, intended to put him on trial, have him face the evidence of what she considered his crime to be.

If Chloe was out here and not at Sand Point, then where was Emma? The large open space of the cabin didn't resemble the room from the picture that Emma had been in.

Madeline's gaze fell and she noticed the twin-size bed was in a weird spot in relation to everything else in the room. As though it should have been pushed against the wall, but instead it was in the middle of the room. She stepped back and lowered to one knee.

One of the legs on the bed was positioned over a door in the floor. Madeline got up and shoved the bed to the side. She tugged on the door handle.

The hatch door lifted, revealing a hanging rope ladder that led to a lit room belowground.

Madeline climbed down, one hand on the ladder and the other planted on the grip of her gun. Halfway on her descent, she turned and came eye to eye with Emma.

A wave of relief swept over Madeline. She'd found her.

The little girl looked so much like Jackson. She was sitting on a bed that had a gray wool blanket, playing with a doll. Her glassy brown eyes flared wide as she pulled her legs up to her chest and drew back against the wall.

"You don't need to be afraid of me, Emma. My name is Madeline," she said, jumping off the ladder and looking the child over. Her face was clean, her hair brushed. Remnants of a sandwich, a bottle of water and a Hershey's bar wrapper were on a small table nearby. "I'm an agent with the FBI. It's like the police. I'm also a friend of your dad. I'm here to help you. To bring you home."

Madeline glanced around the bunker. The floor was concrete, as were the walls. Without the newspaper to hide the fact that the walls were made of bare concrete, it would've been easy to tell that Emma was being kept in a cellar. Or a bunker.

Emma leaped off the bed and ran to Madeline, dropping the doll at her feet. "Where's my daddy?" The girl's voice shook. "I want to go home."

Madeline gathered Emma into a tight hug. "Your dad is waiting for you. He misses you so much."

The girl squeezed back, and an unfamiliar warmth flooded Madeline.

She wasn't used to this struggle to balance her emotions with her job. As though the two had to remain separate in the same manner she held herself apart from everyone. Never allowed herself to get close, to become attached. Until Jackson. For so long she believed cutting herself off was the only way to protect herself when she had only been cheating herself.

Maybe she was strong enough to dedicate herself to a purpose and have a life.

Pulling back from the hug, Madeline took out her phone and thumbed a quick message to Jackson so he'd know Emma was all right.

The message failed to send. No reception, she reminded herself.

Emma tugged on Madeline's jacket. "She'll be back soon," the girl whispered.

"How do you know?"

"She told me that someone was here. To stay quiet while she took a look and that if I didn't, she would hurt Daddy."

Not only was Chloe at the site, but she was aware that Madeline was, too.

Madeline ushered Emma to the ladder. "We're going to get out of here, sweetheart. Right now." She helped the child up, staying behind her on the ladder.

When Madeline climbed out of the bunker back into the room, Emma was staring at the wall with Theon's picture.

"That wasn't there earlier," the little girl said.

Chloe must be close to ending this if she had just hung up her version of evidence.

Madeline took Emma by the hand. "Let's go." They rushed through the door and hurried toward the SUV, but Madeline stopped short.

"What's wrong?" Emma asked. "Why aren't we leaving?"

All four tires were flat. Slashed. And the gate was closed.

They weren't driving out of there.

Chloe was close by. Probably watching them now.

Madeline looked around, scanning the woods,

and hauled the little girl back inside the cabin. "Change of plans, Emma. I have—"

"Striker!" called a woman from outside.

Chloe.

"It's her," Emma said. "We took too long. She's back."

"I know you're in there," Chloe said. "I'm not letting you leave here with Emma. Come out with your hands in the air."

If Madeline went out and exposed herself, she'd be easy pickings. "I don't think so." Better to stay put and wait for Chloe to try to get in.

"Come out now!" Chloe said. "Or I set the cabin on fire."

Emma wrapped her arms around Madeline's waist and clung to her. "I'm scared."

"Shh. It's going to be okay." Madeline stroked her hair, trying to think. "Chloe! I don't think you're going to do that. I know you care about Emma. You don't want anything bad to happen to her. So, why don't you put down any weapons you have and we can talk about this."

"You're right. I don't want to hurt Emma. But if you force me, push me to do it, then I will. Come out, hands up, or you'll regret testing me."

For a strained heartbeat, Madeline closed her eyes, thinking of a solution. A way out of this predicament. But nothing came to her.

"You've got thirty seconds to decide," Chloe

said. "Once the fire starts, I won't be able to stop it."

The car was useless. Without cell reception calling for help was impossible. Madeline couldn't run, not with Emma. It would only expose the child to more danger. The best place for her, the safest place for a little longer, was unfortunately here.

Madeline lifted the hatch to the bunker. "I need you to go back down."

"No!" Emma cried. "Please don't make me. I want to stay with you."

The girl's words tugged at her heart. Kneeling, Madeline brought herself to eye level with the child and rubbed her arms up and down. "I know you do, sweetheart. But it's not safe for you out there. Lots of terrible things that could hurt you. I have to do what she says. It's the only way to keep anything bad from happening to you. Okay?"

Tears rolled down Emma's cheeks, but she nodded. "You'll come back for me, won't you?"

"Time is almost up!" Chloe said.

Madeline wanted to reassure Emma without lying to her. "Help will come. You're not spending another night in that bunker. I promise."

The little girl threw her arms around Madeline's neck and squeezed in a tight hug. "Okay."

Madeline helped her climb back down the ladder.

At the bottom, Emma picked up the doll and clutched it to her chest.

"Don't worry. I always keep my promises." Madeline lowered the door to the bunker and pushed the bed on top of the door. The idea of leaving the girl made her sick and the prospect of Emma escaping, only to get hurt in the woods, was just as horrible.

"Time's up," Chloe said.

"I'm coming out." Madeline opened the cabin door and stepped out slowly with her palms raised. She searched the tree line for Chloe.

The disturbed woman was there. Close. Hiding.

"You are not going to ruin this for me," Chloe said. "I've earned the right to see this through. With my patience. All my planning. There were lots of times in the past two years where I was close enough to Jackson to stick a knife in his throat, poison him or strangle him. I thought about lots of different ways to kill him. But I watched. I listened. Bided my time while learning about his hopes and fears, what he cared about most. Waited for the perfect opportunity to make him pay. And now everything has fallen perfectly into place and no one is going to stop me."

Madeline followed the direction of Chloe's voice and pinpointed the general area the woman was hiding in, but she couldn't spot her. Was she flat on the ground behind a bush? Up in the trees? Her voice carried so much that Madeline couldn't be sure.

"Jackson has paid dearly," Madeline said.

"Not nearly enough. The only thing I regret is not cutting the strings on his piano to take away that bit of solace. But it would've shown my hand, tipped him off to me too fast. And he only would've ordered a new one. Well, he can't order a new CEO position, or stealth technology, or a new daughter."

"Yes, you've hurt him deeply. More than I think you realize. You can stop this now before anyone gets hurt. He has suffered every single minute that Emma has been gone. He's sick with worry and guilt."

Chloe gave a bitter laugh. "Don't lie to me. You can't fool me, Agent Striker. I have cameras hidden in the smoke detectors in his house, watching his every move. I saw the two of you last night. Together. In his bed."

Fury bubbled and spilled over into shock. Then the magnitude of it sunk in, the violation of being watched during a moment of raw intimacy. Madeline swallowed hard against the nausea rising in her throat that made her dizzy.

Sheer force of will alone kept her steady on her feet.

"He didn't look like he was suffering when he was inside you," Chloe said. The derision in her voice cut like a blade.

Clearing her throat, Madeline ignored the sweat chilling her forehead. "It's not too late to stop this."

"But it is. Even if it weren't, why would I stop?"

The bush dead ahead, forty feet away, shook. Madeline itched to draw her weapon, aim and take the shot. End this.

A rabbit darted out from the bush and hopped away.

Damn it. Where was Chloe?

"You're the first woman he's looked at, much less touched, in years," Chloe said. "So, I think it fitting that I use you as practice. For when I bait him to come out here later tonight. You can experience what he's going to feel as I make him run the gauntlet of the Survivalist Zone. I'll make certain that he comes across your dead body and sees you bloody and broken before he draws his last breath."

The one weakness Chloe had in this was her feelings for Emma. Yes, the child was a piece on a chess board to her, but not one she wanted to sacrifice. Somewhere along the way she started to care for her. Madeline had to use that against her.

"What about Emma?" Madeline asked, redirecting the conversation. "If you take away her father, you'll make her an orphan. She'll be all alone. Like you are. You don't want that for her. I know you don't."

"She'll have me. I'll raise her," Chloe said. "Teach her. Love her. She'll barely remember Jackson after a while."

"Chloe, step out where I can see you." Where Madeline could get a solid shot off. "Face to face, we can talk this through. You don't have to do this."

A flicker of movement up in the trees near the entrance drew Madeline's gaze. She spotted Chloe, dark hair pulled back, and wearing some kind of camouflage to help her blend in with the woods.

Madeline caught the flash of an arrow cutting through the air too late.

The arrow struck her left thigh. Madeline screamed in pain, clutching her leg.

"But I do have to do this," Chloe said. "For Theon. For myself. Everything I've planned for so long is working out and I need to finish it. I won't rest until Jackson Rhodes has suffered and lost everything. Including his life. Just like my brother. I'm going to play nice with you, Agent Striker. Give you a sixty-second head start before I hunt you down. Your time begins now."

Was Chloe serious?

Madeline only contemplated it for a second. She took off into the woods in the opposite direction.

Hobbling along with her wounded leg, she bit back a groan of pain.

Chloe had deliberately positioned herself near the entrance to force Madeline deeper into the Survivalist Zone. Not that she would've gotten far down the main road either, not with an arrow in her leg.

If only her cell phone had reception, she could call someone. Tell them. But she was all alone. No one in sight. No one around for miles to help her.

Satellites played no role in cell phone reception, so getting closer to the sky, or getting a clear shot at it, wouldn't necessarily result in a connection. Cellular reception largely depended on how close you were to a cell tower, what man-made obstructions and geographical obstructions stood in between. Like the mountains surrounding her. But a higher elevation might put her in line of sight with a cell tower and help her get that one crucial bar of coverage.

Her only chance, no matter how slim the odds, was to make her way to higher ground and hope for a cell connection.

There was a hill not too far off that might work. She looked around, scouting the best route to the top.

Spears sticking out of a bush on the right had Madeline going left. She picked up her pace, despite the agony lancing through her, knowing that Chloe was close behind.

Her ankle snagged on something. She was

about to look down to see what it was when she heard an earsplitting whoosh.

Without thinking, Madeline dropped to the ground as a heavy log swung out with tremendous force, slicing through the air where she had just been standing.

If she hadn't dropped, she could've been killed instantly, or suffered such traumatic internal injuries that she would've died slowly. But the pain that wrenched through her leg stole her breath.

With her eyes tearing up and heart throbbing, Madeline rolled onto her back and snapped the shaft of the arrow in half. She reached out, grabbing hold of a stick that was long enough to use as a cane and scrambled up from the ground.

She stumbled forward, pulling her gun from the holster in case Chloe popped up unexpectedly. It was only a matter of time before she did.

Determined to move faster, she dug in with the stick and hopped up the hill, doing what she could not to put too much weight on her bleeding leg.

Madeline funneled her anger and pain and used it to fuel her onward. To push uphill with everything that she had. She limped faster, breathing hard. Tuned out the pain from her wound and the ache from her muscles. Breath sawed in and out of her lungs. She was nearly to the top.

Dropping the stick, she pulled out her phone, keeping her gun in her other hand.

Almost there. Almost.

Madeline kept going, climbing up the hill. She just needed to reach the top, get a signal and call for help. Tell them where Emma was and make sure this area was surrounded before Liane or Chloe or whatever the hell her name was could get away.

Certain her assailant was on her tail, she darted in between trees. Stayed low.

Looking down at the phone, she checked it for bars. Nothing. Not yet. She cut between pine trees, darting behind them and crawling over fallen logs, scrambling ever higher up the hill.

Her phone chimed.

Madeline stopped and looked at her cell. Two bars.

The message she had typed earlier went through. She went to press the call icon when an arrow whizzed past her head, hitting the trunk of the pine beside her.

She looked downhill. Spotted Chloe moving like a shadow between the trees. A ghillie suit helped to conceal her.

Madeline fired twice at the woman, forcing her to duck. Then she hurried higher.

But she had to keep track of Chloe. Risking a glance back, Madeline twisted her ankle on a rock. A new type of pain ricocheted along her shin. *Oh, God.* She tried to find her footing and landed wrong, tripping on a tree limb, throwing her forward as her knees buckled.

The ground gave way beneath her feet.

Her arms flailed. She desperately sought to grab hold of something. Anything to keep from falling. The phone and gun dropped from her hands as she snatched onto thick vines at the edge of the pit, breaking her fall.

THE KIDNAPPER WAS inside Jackson's head, playing a sick, twisted game of manipulation.

Behind the wheel of his Tesla, he ran through the what-ifs. What if he did as the note instructed, yet again? Ditched the FBI and went rogue? Why would the outcome be any different this time? What if the person never had any intention of giving Emma back? What if this was another power move designed to hurt him, physically this time?

The more he thought about it and calculated the risks, there was only one thing he could do. Discuss it with Madeline. She had been right about so many other things. The smart, tough agent would help him figure out what to do.

In the meantime, he needed to make sure she got back safely.

Jackson drove down the 405, headed for the Survivalist Zone site. Madeline had no idea how dangerous the place was. From intricate booby traps to the rugged terrain that could flatten a tire. Not to mention there might be wildlife on the property.

She didn't fully understand what she was walking into, and he did.

Jackson glanced at the gun case on the passenger seat. Mountain lions and snakes posed as much of a threat as any of the man-made hazards.

His phone chimed. A new message.

Cold dread fisted in his chest. If it was another text from the kidnapper, tormenting him, taunting him, pushing up the deadline to meet, he didn't know what he'd do.

He took out his phone. It was from Madeline, not an unknown number.

Sucking in a breath, he swiped the screen and looked at the message.

Found Emma in the bunker at the SZ site. She's unharmed. Chloe Lasiter is Liane Strothe.

His mouth dried as relief tangled with disbelief.

Thank, God. Emma was alive and all right.

His thoughts circled back to Liane. Chloe Lasiter was Liane. A woman he had trusted, who he had let into his home.

All this time, she'd been watching him, spying on him, plotting how to best hurt him. *For two damn years!*

Tension bled through him, tightening every muscle in his body. Pressure built in his chest so fast and hard, for a second he thought he was having a heart attack.

Jackson dialed Madeline, but the call didn't connect. *And Liane, what about her?* What if she was still in the area, out at the site?

A million terrible possibilities spun in his mind.

Getting into the Survivalist Zone site was one thing. Getting out could be an entirely different situation, especially if Liane—Chloe—one of the masterminds behind the design, was out there.

Rage replaced everything else and it was like acid burning in his veins. Jackson pressed harder on the accelerator, changing lanes to veer away from a slow-moving minivan. He dialed the BAU office. It rang and rang.

Come on. Someone pick up.

"Liam McDare. How can I help you?"

Weaving around traffic, he cut off a sedan and took the exit ramp off the 405 and gunned it. "This is Jackson Rhodes. I heard from Madeline. She found Emma at an old ETC site that had been used by Theon Lasiter." He relayed how to get there. "I haven't been able to reach Madeline, but I'm on my way out there now."

Chapter Sixteen

Had a vine not been handy, Madeline would've fallen into the pit. Her heart pounded in her throat as she held on for dear life. She looked down. Wooden spikes pointed up from the ground. Her phone and gun had both fallen and were three feet below her. Dropping down to get them wasn't a viable possibility. Her feet or a limb would land on a spike. There were too many to avoid.

Even if she somehow managed to drop down safely to get her phone and gun, she'd be trapped. A sitting duck for Chloe.

She tugged on the vines, and using all her upper-body strength, pulled herself up. One hand over the other. She pushed up from the ground, and forced herself to bend her injured leg, swallowed a scream.

Breathing through the hot vise of pain gripping her leg, Madeline glanced around. No sign of Chloe. But she couldn't sit there waiting for her.

Level ground was best for her leg. She had to get off the hill.

Birds flew out of a tree twenty feet away as though something had spooked them.

Every sense she had went into overdrive as the need to survive took over.

Run!

Madeline scrambled in the opposite direction. Headed back downhill.

Keep moving. Don't stop.

Run as fast as you can!

Another arrow whistled through the air, landing in bark inches from her head.

Oh, God.

Madeline ducked low, but didn't stop. She gasped for air, her mind racing like a mouse caught in a maze. There had to be a way to save herself and Emma. To make sure Chloe never had a chance to drive Jackson through this gauntlet of hell and misery.

Chloe was closing in on her. She could feel it. There wasn't much time.

In a physical struggle with Chloe while injured, she wouldn't win. Since she'd lost her gun, she had no weapon aside from what she might be able to find. A tree branch maybe.

She had to outwit Chloe. Somehow. Keep moving. Hope her text message had gotten through and Jackson had notified the BAU team. She doubled back toward the cabin instead of finding out what was in store deeper in the zone.

Heart throbbing as if it would burst, she slogged forward to God only knew where. Chloe had been over every inch of this land, knew it, had it memorized.

Despite the pain searing through her body, Madeline ran onward. Hard. Limping and bleeding.

She found herself near the area where she had started.

Her gaze snagged on the spears sticking out of the bush. Seeing the bush before had driven her away from it in the opposite direction, toward a trap. Maybe that's why it was visible. But maybe she could use this to her advantage.

She hobbled to the bush. Grabbing onto one of the spears, she wiggled it and pried it loose. Now that she had a weapon, she needed to find someplace to hide.

Crossing a stream, she passed a tight cluster of trees and came to thick underbrush. She bent down, gritting her teeth when she wanted to scream, and crawled into a bush.

She'd have to be cautious. Listen for even the snap of a twig around her. She could do this. Had to. She was out of other options. This was the best one.

Better to try anything than let that psychopath kill her.

Fury burned through Madeline.

Bring it on, Chloe.

I won't go down without a fight!

JACKSON DROVE AS close as he dared to the entrance of the Survivalist Zone. He parked behind a stand of pine and grabbed the loaded gun from the case. Then with an eye on the locked gate, he crept through the woods in its direction.

He spotted the government SUV. His heart leaped, but there was no sign of Madeline.

Nothing moved around the cabin. No one passed in the dark windows. No smoke curled from the chimney.

With his nerves singing, he entered the code at the gate. The lock disengaged.

He slipped inside, closing it slowly, quietly behind him.

Passing the SUV, he noticed the tires had been slashed. All of them.

He made his way to the front door, careful of where he stepped, and edged inside the cabin. Glancing around, he caught sight of Theon's picture on the wall. But he didn't want to look at it. Theon was gone. As tragic as his suicide was, he was gone. Emma was alive. And here somewhere. That's all he cared about it. Finding his little girl and Madeline and getting them both out safely.

Jackson walked through the room, searching

for a sign that Emma had been in the cabin. A floorboard creaked. He stopped and walked back over it.

Staring at the floor, he remembered. Theon had constructed a bunker. Concrete walls. Concrete floor. Like the room Emma was being held hostage in.

Jackson kicked the bed aside. Found the door and opened the hatch. He climbed onto the ladder, got down two rungs and jumped down the rest of the way, sending a pang through him.

He spun around and the air caught in his lungs. *Emma!*

"Daddy!" Emma raced to him and launched herself into his arms.

Ignoring the pain slicing through his side, he wrapped his little girl in the biggest, tightest hug. "Oh, baby!" He kissed her head, her cheeks, her hair. *But where was Madeline?* "Honey, have you seen anyone else besides Liane? Did a nice woman find you?"

"Madeline?"

He set his daughter down. "Yes. Do you know what happened to her?"

Emma shook her head. "Liane made her go outside and Madeline told me it was safer to stay down here. She promised help would come. She was right." His daughter wrapped her arms around his neck.

Despite the pain, Jackson lifted her in his

arms. He'd gladly endure any discomfort if it meant he could hold his child.

He climbed out of the bunker. Opening the door, he peeked outside.

"You can't hide from me!" Chloe said in the distance. "Come out and I'll make it quick. If I have to find you myself, it'll be slow and painful, Agent Striker."

Madeline is in trouble.

Jackson darted out of the cabin, making his way back through the gate. This time he left it cracked open. Down the road, he cut into the trees to his car. He opened the back door and placed Emma inside.

"I need you to be a brave girl for me. A little longer. Stay down in the footwell." He grabbed the blanket from the seat that he always kept in the car and covered her with it. "Daddy's friend Madeline is in danger. I have to help her. Liane wants to hurt her."

"But she wants to hurt you, too."

That woman already had. "I know, baby. But I'm going to be careful. Stay here until I come back or the police arrive. Don't move for any other reason. Understand, darling?"

"You can't hide from me!" Chloe said, her voice circling closer. "Come out and I'll make it quick. If I have to find you myself, it'll be slow and painful, Agent Striker."

Slow and painful it would be unless Madeline killed her first because there was no way in hell she was surrendering.

Something moved on the ground, underneath the same bush. A squirrel? Maybe a rabbit.

No, it was smaller.

Madeline didn't dare move an inch to see what it was, praying it would crawl or scamper off. But it didn't. It slithered closer.

A snake! Madeline swore in her head. She hated snakes, was terrified of them. But in terms of things to fear, Chloe was higher on the list.

Squeezing her eyes shut, she sucked in a calming breath. She hoped, prayed, it would slither past. Most of the snakes in Washington were nonvenomous. Not a concern. The only one she needed to worry about was—

A distinct rattle clacked under the bush.

Madeline gulped hard around the lump of ice in her throat. A rattlesnake was cause for concern. It could kill her. Not on the spot. Pain and swelling would start at the wound site and travel and spread from there.

With Chloe stalking her, there was only one thing Madeline could do.

Killing the rattlesnake wasn't an option. Crawling to a new hiding spot wasn't an option.

She braced herself as the snake slithered closer. The sound of the rattle filled her ears along with the frantic drum of her heart.

The sting was vicious. Brutal. But the rattler sank its fangs into her ankle twice. The second bite caught her off guard. Though she swallowed her cry, she'd jerked back, shaking the bush.

Chloe lunged into the underbrush, snatching Madeline by the hair, and dragged her out.

Screaming, Madeline rammed the spear up into flesh with all her might. She didn't stop thrusting the sharpened pole into the woman until Chloe let her go.

Madeline's vision blurred. She tried to stand, but the leg the snake had bitten turned to jelly, and the other, wounded from the arrow, was too weak to support her, so she crashed to the ground. Her thighs and calves were aching in agony, her lungs on fire. Rolling on her back to keep Chloe in her sights, Madeline shuffled backward. But there was nowhere to go. Nowhere to hide. She couldn't even run.

Chloe's lips curled, baring her teeth in a face smudged with camouflage. The woman reached behind her, pulling something from the pack strapped on her back. A weapon. She held a rope, and on the end dangled a rock with spikes ducttaped around it.

Adrenaline sent Madeline scurrying away, scooting across the ground until a tree stopped her retreat. She swung the spear, desperate to keep Chloe at a distance.

The woman dodged the last wild swing of the

spear and kicked Madeline in the leg injured from the arrow.

Madeline screamed, but swung the spear again at her attacker.

Chloe whipped the spiked rock in the air, faster and faster, picking up speed and gaining momentum. She launched the weapon and with a powerful whack split the spear in two.

The crunch of the wood splintering resonated in Madeline's soul.

"It's over, Agent Striker!" Teeth bared and growling like a wild beast, Chloe started swinging the spiked rock again. Preparing to strike Madeline in the leg. Or chest. Or the face.

A wave of horrifying panic engulfed her. In a frantic last-ditch effort, Madeline kicked at her. With her dying breath, she'd fight. "Go to hell!"

Chloe raised the spiked rock over her head and swung.

Boom!

The report of the 9 mm sounded like a cannon explosion, so loud it rattled Madeline's teeth. She froze, confused. Dazed.

Chloe's eyes went blank as she dropped to her knees dead before she keeled over to the ground.

Jackson rushed to Madeline, lowering to a knee. He pressed a hand to her cheek, his frantic gaze traveling over her body. "Are you okay?"

"Emma," she said, her throat tight and sore. "Did you find Emma?"

"Yes, yes. She's safe."

A helicopter flew overhead and circled back, setting down near the cabin.

She rested her head on Jackson's shoulder and looked at the body.

It was finally finished.

Chloe Lasiter was dead.

Epilogue

Three days later...

Most of the team took up every available seat in Miguel's hospital room while they enjoyed dinner together and kept him company for a little while. The only person missing was Caitlyn, who was on a date.

Madeline's thigh and ankle both throbbed, but the soreness had improved considerably after the first couple of days.

"I wish I could've brought him in alive," Miguel said, referring to the terrorist suspect he'd had to shoot.

"We all read your report," Nick said. "You didn't have a choice."

Dash nodded. "The guy had a gun to the kid's head. You had a split second to make the right call and you did. You saved a life."

"But I wanted to bring him to justice," Miguel said. "Squeeze him for information that could've ended up saving even more lives."

"We're just glad you're going to be all right," Madeline said.

"And you as well." Miguel glanced at her leg.

"I'm okay. Compared to you getting shot, this is like a scratch," Madeline said, downplaying her injury, not liking the attention, but it was also true.

Unlike Madeline, it would be a week before Miguel would be back on his feet and another two before they'd see him in the office.

"I read your report, too," Miguel said. "You almost didn't make it out of the Survivalist Zone."

A shiver ran through her thinking how close Chloe had gotten to almost ending her life. But thanks to Jackson, that disturbed woman had failed.

For once, Madeline was glad he didn't listen to her and *had* gone rogue. If he hadn't already been on his way out to the site to help her before he'd gotten her text message, he never would have made it there in time to save her life. For a second time.

"Jackson and I ended up making a good unofficial team and saved his daughter." She smiled, though her chest ached from not having heard from Jackson.

Not that she had any expectations. No strings attached.

Yet deep in the recesses of her heart she had

hoped, foolishly, that once Emma was safe, he might still be interested in her.

But there had been nothing but silence between them. Even thinking of it now, no call, no text, something inside her withered.

Shoving the thought aside and tamping down the prickle of disappointment, she turned to Liam. With his head hung and pushing his food around in his take-out container, he hadn't spoken much.

"Liam, have you and Lorelai not worked things out yet?" she asked.

He clenched his jaw and shook his head. "I messed up. A part of me was afraid to go through with it and walk down the aisle. I mean, look at my parents. Even Lorelai's folks are divorced. But now that the wedding is off…" Shrugging, he slapped his container closed. "Careful what you wish for because you just might get it."

"This isn't all your fault," Madeline said. "A relationship takes two people, and I will admit to you, because I've already done so directly to Lorelai, that she was becoming a bit of a bridezilla."

The others in the room nodded emphatically.

"It's going to be okay," Nick said.

Dash patted him on the back. "Whatever is supposed to happen, will."

"If you miss her and want to work it out," Miguel said, "then you can. One thing I know for certain is that life is too short to let an opportunity for love pass you by."

ON THE DRIVE HOME, Madeline couldn't get Miguel's words out of her head. He was right. Life was too short to let an opportunity for love and happiness pass by. But it took mutual interest, mutual attraction, mutual desire on the parts of both parties. She couldn't force something that wasn't there, no matter how much she wanted Jackson.

Funny, she'd gone all these years content to be on her own, and after knowing him a few short days, he'd turned her world upside down. Had her reevaluating what she wanted, needed. Made her consider facing her fear of attachment rather than running from it.

In her condo, she kicked off her shoes and poured a glass of wine since she no longer needed her pain medication. She pulled the pins from her hair and took down the loose twist. Sipping a glass of cabernet, she figured she'd take a bath and curl up with a book tonight.

The doorbell rang.

She groaned, realizing it was that time of year again when kids went knocking door-to-door selling candy to raise funds for their school.

"One minute." She set her glass down, grabbed her checkbook and opened the door.

Her heart flipped over.

Jackson and Emma.

The two of them stood hand in hand, smiling. No, beaming at her.

"What are you doing here?" she asked, hearing the words that left her mouth and regretting them when his smile faltered. "I mean, I'm surprised you're here. But glad." Jump-up-and-down ecstatic.

"We both wanted to see you," Jackson said. "Can we come in?"

"Of course." She opened the door wide. "Please."

"How are—?" she and Jackson said at the same time and laughed.

"I'm good," she said. "Your ribs?"

"Still healing and Emma is sleeping through the night now and back in her own bed."

Emma held out a card. "This is for you. I made it."

"Thank you." Madeline took the piece of folded construction paper and stared at the flowers and rainbow drawn on the cover. Inside was a smiley face inside a heart. Emma had scribbled, "Thank you for saving me." Emotion clogged Madeline's throat and she couldn't speak as surprising tears wet her eyes. "It's so beautiful. I'll treasure it."

The little girl gave Madeline a hug, and she bent down to tighten the embrace.

"Emma, why don't you go sit on the sofa for a minute while Madeline and I talk?" He handed her a kiddie tablet, and she went to the couch.

"How did you know where I lived?" Madeline asked.

"Caitlyn took pity on me and told me. I hope that's okay. I wanted to talk to you in person, not over the phone or at your office."

She owed Caitlyn one. "It's fine. I don't mind."

"I wanted to come sooner, but I needed to focus on Emma. Make sure she was all right."

"She's your number-one priority. I get that."

"I can't stop thinking about you. I know big, important things about you, but I want to know more. Everything. The name of your third-grade teacher, your favorite dessert, your happiest memory. What your go-to takeout is."

"Sushi. Spicy scallop roll and tuna *tataki*."

"That's a start." He stepped closer. "Caitlyn also mentioned that you're taking a couple of days off. I was wondering if you'd like to come to dinner with me and Emma, tomorrow night. In Paris."

"Paris?" She owed Caitlyn big-time!

"Why not? You'll be on vacation and I'm not currently employed."

"You're not going back to ETC?"

"I don't know. I want to take some time. Spend it with Emma. And you." He cupped her jaw and caressed her cheek with his thumb.

She was surprised by the sudden twist of desire that stabbed through her, all the way from her scalp to the pit of her stomach. It took her breath away, and she wanted him with a force that frightened her.

"What do you say about Paris?"

"I'd love to, Jack."

* * * * *

Look for Trapping a Terrorist
*by Caridad Piñeiro, the final book in
the Behavioral Analysis Unit series,
available next month.*

*And don't miss the previous
books in the series:*

Profiling a Killer *by Nichole Severn*
Decoding a Criminal *by Barb Han*

*Both are available now wherever
Harlequin Intrigue books are sold!*

Get 4 FREE REWARDS!

We'll send you 2 FREE Books plus 2 FREE Mystery Gifts.

Harlequin Romantic Suspense books are heart-racing page-turners with unexpected plot twists and irresistible chemistry that will keep you guessing to the very end.

FREE Value Over $20

Get 4 FREE REWARDS!

We'll send you 2 FREE Books plus 2 FREE Mystery Gifts.

Harlequin Presents books feature the glamorous lives of royals and billionaires in a world of exotic locations, where passion knows no bounds.

FREE Value Over $20

Get 4 FREE REWARDS!

We'll send you 2 FREE Books plus <u>2 FREE Mystery Gifts.</u>

Worldwide Library books feature gripping mysteries from "whodunits" to police procedurals and courtroom dramas.

FREE
Value Over
$20